The Hit

A Chilling T[

By Ditter Kellen

www.ditterkellen.com

Copyright © Ditter Kellen

All rights reserved. This copy is intended for the original purchaser of this book ONLY. No part of this book may be reproduced, scanned, or distributed in any printed or electronic form without prior written permission from Ditter Kellen. Please do not participate in or encourage piracy of copyrighted materials in violation of the author's rights. Purchase only authorized editions.

Image/art disclaimer: Licensed material is being used for illustrative purposes only. Any person depicted in the licensed material is a model.

Published in the United States of America.

Ditter Kellen

P.O. Box 1088

Bonifay, FL. 32425

This book is a work of fiction. While reference might be made to actual historical events or existing locations, the names, characters, places and incidents are either the product of the author's imagination or are used fictitiously, and any resemblance to actual persons, living or dead, business establishments, events, or locales are entirely coincidental.

Warning

This book contains graphic scenes that may be considered offensive to some readers.

Dedication

For my beautiful friend, Tina Barker, a lady I met years ago when I worked as a 911 dispatcher in Florida. Tina was my supervisor. We became close and have remained so since. She is extremely intelligent and handles herself well under pressure. Though I only get to see her on rare occasions when I visit Florida, I will love her always.

I hope she enjoys this twisted tale of murder and mayhem as much as I enjoyed spinning it.

Acknowledgment

A big thank-you to my bestie and beta reader, Cathe Green, for her guidance, patience, and unending friendship. I'll never be able to repay her for all her help when I'm mucking my way through the madness. I love you!

Mike Barker, Tina's handsome husband, was the perfect man to play Tina's significant other in the book. I appreciate him allowing me to write him into the insanity. He's such a good sport!

Roslynn Ernst is an online friend I met several years ago, who reads my books and has always been such a pleasure. Thank you for allowing me to mutilate you in the story. Ha-ha. Love you, lady!

Bobbi Laroche is a local-to-me reader who I connected with on Facebook. She's a sweetheart of a lady, and I can't wait to meet her in person!

Karen Harper Hawkins and I have been online friends for many years. She lives halfway across the world from me, which makes meeting in person almost a distant dream. Maybe one day. Love you, Karen!

Desiree Leonard... I hope you enjoy your role as one of Bay County's investigators. You're a sweetheart. Thank you for being so great.

Renee Clarity is the beautiful daughter of a close friend of mine. I wanted to surprise her with a part in the story. I hope she enjoys!

Chapter One

Tina Duggar stood next to her longtime boyfriend, Mike Parker, as he stared dry-eyed at his father's coffin.

The cemetery remained eerily quiet, save for the deep timbre of the officiating reverend's voice.

Thunder suddenly rolled in the distance, signaling the arrival of an impending storm.

Tina eased her hand over, sliding her palm against Mike's.

He accepted her show of support without question, gently squeezing her fingers in return.

She knew his father's death affected him more than he let on. No matter how aloof he attempted to appear.

Her gaze touched on the small, unmoving crowd gathered around before settling on the red-rimmed eyes of Mike's stepmother.

It wasn't lost on Tina that Mike hadn't offered his condolences to the grieving widow. Not that Tina blamed him. The woman had been to blame for wrecking Mike's home all those years ago.

Mike's father, Gerald Parker, hadn't been the best father. Not by a long shot. He'd been absent most of Mike's life and, more often than not, forgot his only son's birthday. Not to mention his graduation.

Gerald had owned half the car dealerships in Bay County, Florida, which had left him extremely well off and more than a little cynical. Money and power had been the most important things to Gerald. That, and women.

Tina's thoughts drifted to Mike's mother. The woman had died still loving Gerald, even though he'd left her years ago for a much younger woman. And therein lay the root of Mike's anger toward the man.

Stepping in closer, Tina ran her thumb along Mike's knuckles. The show of support elicited the desired response.

Mike glanced down at her, a look of gratefulness shining from his hazel-colored eyes.

He had to be the most handsome man Tina had ever seen. There was just something about him that held her captivated, something that ran deeper than the physical. He had an intelligence and gentleness that drew her in. But it was his alpha core that had sealed her fate.

The reverend finished speaking and backed up a step while nodding to Gerald's window. The woman scooped up a handful of dirt and sprinkled it on top of the coffin.

Mike followed suit without releasing Tina's hand. He then turned and walked away.

Tina trailed along next to him. "Are you okay?"

A muscle ticked along his jaw, an obvious sign of the emotion he attempted to hide.

He opened his mouth to answer but was interrupted by a short, balding man in an obviously expensive suit.

"Mr. Parker?"

Mike stopped to face the man, keeping Tina close at his side. "Yes?"

"My name is Allen Tindale," the man greeted, extending his hand and glancing in the direction of Mike's stepmother. "I'm your father's attorney."

Tina remained quiet as Mike accepted the man's palm. "Thank you for coming, Mr. Tindale."

"Of course." The attorney cleared his throat, continuing without preamble. "I realize this isn't the best time, Mr. Parker, but I'm leaving for Italy tomorrow, and I'd like to meet with you to discuss your father's will." He nervously flicked his gaze in the widow's direction once more.

Tina gently disengaged her hand from Mike's. "I'll just give you two a minute. I'll be in the car."

Mike sent her a nod, his focus returning to his father's attorney.

Tina could hear them speaking low as she made her way toward the vehicles on the outskirts of the cemetery.

Fishing the keys from her skirt pocket, she unlocked Mike's car doors and slipped inside.

Her cell phone lay on the console between the seats. She plucked it up and swiped her thumb across the screen. There were three text messages from Roslynn Earnhardt, one of Tina's longtime friends.

Checking the first one, Tina silently read, *Have fun in Orlando this weekend.*

The second text appeared to have arrived six minutes after the first one. *Call me if you get a chance. I'm in town for a week, so hopefully I'll see you when you return from your trip.*

Deleting the first two, Tina read the last one. *BTW, my days as a traveling nurse are coming to an end. Starting next year, I'll be officially working from Bay County. Yay! Talk soon.*

Tina hit reply. *At a funeral. Will call you soon!*

The driver's side door opened, and Mike slid behind the wheel. He sat there for long moments without speaking. And then, "Something's come up. I'm not going to make Orlando, babe. I'm so sorry."

Tina reached across the seat and laid her hand on his arm. "Don't apologize. You just lost your father. The trip can be rescheduled. I—"

"No," he gently interrupted, sending her an apologetic look. "Don't cancel the trip. You've been looking forward to it for months. Go and have a good time. Take a friend with you. There's just something I need to take care of."

Tina stared into his eyes. "Is everything all right?"

Mike blew out a breath. "My father's attorney wants to go over the will with me. He's leaving tomorrow and likely won't be back for a couple of months. I wasn't expecting to have to deal with this so soon."

Cranking the car, Mike closed his door and drove away from the cemetery.

They rode in silence for several minutes before Tina spoke. "I don't feel right about leaving you at a time like this."

"Listen to me," Mike began, turning onto Tina's street, "I haven't seen my father in more than twelve years. It's not as if we were close. I'm fine. I promise. But I have a feeling I'm going to be wrapped up all weekend. There's no sense in you canceling the trip because of me."

The sudden death of Gerald Parker hadn't seemed to phase Mike. But Tina wasn't fooled by his show of bravado. Deep down, it affected him. She had felt it back at that cemetery.

She studied his profile before forcing her attention back to the road. Perhaps he was right. Maybe he needed some time alone to process his father's passing. The man had only been fifty-seven years old. Much too young to die.

Chapter Two

Tina emerged from the shower, wrapped her hair in a towel, and tugged on her robe. Mike had dropped her off over an hour ago and had left to meet with Allen Tindale about Gerald's will.

Blowing out a wistful sigh, she picked up her cell phone and called Roslynn.

"Hello?"

"Hi, Roz, it's Tina."

A brief pause ensued. "Hey, girl. Is everything okay? I got your text that you were at a funeral."

"I'm fine. Mike's dad passed away suddenly."

"Oh my goodness," Roslynn softly exclaimed. "I'm so sorry. What happened?"

"He had a heart attack while in a business meeting."

Roslynn made a soft sound in the back of her throat. "How is Mike taking it?"

Tina trailed to her room to sit on the foot of her bed. "He's handling it pretty well. He and his father were never close. In fact, they haven't spoken in over twelve years."

Tina spent the next ten minutes filling Roslynn in on everything she knew about Mike's relationship with his estranged father. "Mike's with his dad's attorney now, going over the will. Which brings me to my next question. What are you doing this weekend?"

"Going to the beach with Bobbi, if she's not on call. Why, what's up?"

"I believe Bill is on call this weekend," Tina answered, opening the calendar on her phone.

Being the supervisor of Bay County Animal Control, Tina was responsible for making the schedule. And since Bobbi happened to be an animal control officer with the same county, Tina would know when she worked. "Bobbi is off this weekend. How would you guys like to go with me to Universal Studios?"

Roslynn hesitated. "Are you sure?"

"Of course I'm sure. I really don't want to go alone. And since Mike won't be coming…"

"I would love to," Roslynn admitted. "I'll call Bobbi and see if she's available. Talk soon."

Tina ended the call and headed back to the bathroom to dry her hair.

Guilt ate at her for planning a trip without Mike. Especially with the recent turn of events. But Mike needed some space for a few days. He'd made that clear.

* * * *

Tina's cell phone buzzed just as she finished applying her lipstick. She swiped her thumb across the screen to find a text from Roz. *Bobbi is a go. Pick us up at her place?*

Be there in twenty mins, Tina sent back, tucking her phone into the back pocket of her jeans and switching off the bathroom light.

After double-checking her small house to be sure she hadn't forgotten anything, she picked up her suitcase and headed out to her car.

Unlocking the door, she loaded her bags into the trunk of her SUV and put in a call to Mike.

"Hey, babe," he rumbled, picking up on the second ring. "You headed out?"

Tina climbed behind the wheel and started the engine. Putting on her seatbelt, she backed out of the drive. "I am. Are you sure you can't come with me?"

A sigh came through the line. "I'm sure. It seems I've inherited four car dealerships and my father's house."

Tina's eyebrows shot up. "Wow. He left you everything? What about his wife?"

"According to his attorney, she'd signed a prenuptial agreement before they married."

That caught Tina off guard. "Really? Wow. So she got nothing." It wasn't a question.

"She showed up at Tindale's office for the reading of the will," Mike admitted in a weary voice. "Suffice it to say, she wasn't happy. Gerald left her the belongings in the house, twenty-five thousand dollars, and the car in her possession. Nothing more. Nothing less."

They grew quiet for a moment, and then Mike broke the silence. "I'm sorry again about bailing on you this weekend."

Tina's heart squeezed. She hated to leave without him as well. "It's fine, love. Roslynn and Bobbi are going with me. I'm heading to Bobbi's to pick them up now."

"It makes me feel better that you're not going alone. There are too many nutjobs out there."

Tina didn't bother telling him not to worry. Mike Parker had been a seasoned investigator with Bay County for the past ten years. It was in his nature to worry.

Tina thought about the first time she'd met Mike. She had hired on with the sheriff's department as a dispatcher for animal control, when she'd taken a call about possible dog fighting going on in the county.

After several arrests were made, Mike had been the investigator assigned to the case. He had stepped into dispatch to get a copy of the recorded call and left with Tina's heart. That had been almost three years ago.

"Tina?"

"I'm sorry. I was just thinking about the first time we met."

He laughed softly. "When you spilled your coffee on my shirt?"

"Yes." The corner of her mouth lifted at the memory of that day. "In my defense, you *were* hovering."

"I was not hovering," he refuted with a chuckle. "I was merely observing."

Tina outright laughed. "Whatever you say, freak. That's not what I remember."

"I miss you already."

Mike's softly spoken words turned Tina's stomach to mush. "I can stay. I—"

"No," he quickly interrupted. "I have too much going on. Seriously. Please just go and have a good time. You and I will spend a nice, romantic weekend in New Orleans once I get all this stuff settled. I love you."

Tina's heart ached to hold him. "I love you too, Mike. Always."

He ended the call.

Chapter Three

Tina helped Bobbi load her bags into the back of the SUV while Roslynn stacked pillows and blankets onto the third-row seat.

"This thing is going to burn some serious fuel," Roslynn pointed out. "But it sure is roomy."

Tina slammed the hatch shut. "Well, it was a gift from my parents. So, what I pay in gas, I more than make up for in not having a car payment."

"True that." Roslynn readily agreed, climbing into the back seat.

Bobbi rounded the large SUV and hopped into the passenger side.

Tina got behind the wheel, fastened her seatbelt, and adjusted the rearview mirror. "Got everything?"

"I'm good," Roslynn called from the second-row seat. "I double-checked twice before you arrived. Actually, I hadn't unpacked yet, so it was fairly easy for me."

Tina glanced over at Bobbi, who was frantically rummaging through her purse. "What did you forget?"

"I can't find my— Oh, there it is!" Bobbi pulled out a tube of Chapstick and held it up. "Okay, I'm ready."

Roslynn laughed from her position in the back seat. "I can't remember a time when you weren't applying that stuff. You do know that it contains an ingredient that ultimately dries out your lips, forcing you to have a continuous need for it, right?"

"I know," Bobbi responded with a shrug. "But I can't handle dry lips in the meantime."

Tina grinned and started the engine. She backed out of Bobbi's driveway. "I appreciate you guys coming with me to Orlando. I really wasn't looking forward to making the trip alone."

"No need for thanks," Bobbi answered, applying her Chapstick. "You have no idea how much I needed to get away for a few days."

But Tina did know. Joey, Bobbi's alcoholic husband, had been drinking again. According to Bobbi, Joey had been sober for the past two years. Until his job laid him off. He'd fallen off the wagon less than a week later. "Things still bad at home?"

A shadow passed through Bobbi's dark-brown eyes. "They are. But I really don't want to talk about Joey. I just want to have a nice, relaxing weekend with my besties. I'll deal with reality when we get back."

"Enough said." Tina switched on the radio, settling on an eighties rock station.

"What about you?" Roslynn called out over the music.

Tina turned down the volume. "What do you mean?"

"How are things going with you and Mike?"

Tina met Roslynn's gaze in the mirror. "He's the best thing that's ever happened to me."

"Lucky you," Roslynn teased, smiling at Tina's reflection. "The best thing I've ever found was a month-long fling I had with a doctor in North Carolina."

Bobbi turned in her seat to face Roslynn. "You never told me about that. What happened?"

"I discovered he had a wife and kids," Roslynn admitted, a touch of bitterness lining her voice. "And that ended that."

Tina's heart went out to the pretty brunette. She couldn't imagine discovering that Mike was married. "I'm sorry, Roz. Someone will come along one day that's completely right for you. You'll see."

"Roz will step over a good one to get to a bad one," Bobbi pointed out with a chuckle. "She always has."

Roslynn laughed as well. "I do not."

"Yes you do," Tina piped in. "You have the absolute worst taste in men."

Running a hand through her hair, Roslynn shot back, "It's not my taste in men that's off kilter. It's my judgment. I can't see beyond my hormones to recognize the warning signs. I'm weak where they are concerned. Always have been. My mother thinks I'm a bum magnet. If there was a bum within a fifty-mile radius of me, he'd gravitate towards me."

Everyone grew quiet for a moment, and then Tina said, "You're not weak, Roz. You're just too giving. Your heart is the size of Texas. And that's one of the things I love most about you."

"I love you too, Tina Bina."

Tina winked at Roz in the mirror and took the onramp for Interstate 10 to Orlando. A weekend at Universal Studios was just what Roz needed.

Chapter Four

"I really have to pee," Bobbi stated for the third time.

Tina side-eyed her auburn-haired friend. "The next exit is nine miles away. You should have gone when we pulled in to get gas."

"I didn't have to go then." Bobbi suddenly pointed. "There's a rest area up ahead. I can go there."

Tina flipped on her blinker and eased over to the right lane. "We haven't even reached Interstate 75, and you've had to pee three times."

Bobbi grinned. "It's all the soda I had."

"No more soda for you," Roslynn announced, her reflection appearing in the rearview mirror. "But since we're stopping, I need to pee also."

Tina swallowed back a laugh. "Fine. We'll all go at the rest area."

Slowing at the offramp, Tina guided the SUV through the maze that was the rest area. She passed the dog-walking park, pulling to a stop next to a dark-blue sedan with the hood up.

She switched off the engine, grabbed her keys, and got out. Bobbi and Roslynn followed suit.

"I forgot my purse." Roslynn sighed, holding out her hand for the keys.

Tina dropped them onto her palm. "Be sure to lock it back up. All of our stuff is in there."

"Of course." Roslynn spun on her heel.

Once Tina and Bobbi took care of their needs, they moved to the row of sinks to wash their hands.

Tina turned on the water. "I wonder what's taking Roz so long?"

"She's probably looking for her purse. I'm willing to bet she left it at home."

They both chuckled a moment before switching off the water and drying their hands.

Opening the bathroom door, Tina noticed Roslynn standing next to a man, both of them leaning over the hood of the blue sedan parked next to her SUV. "What on earth is she doing?"

Bobbi grinned. "Flirting. Well, he does have a rather nice backside."

"You're a married woman," Tina playfully scolded, her gaze lowering to the man's rear against her will. It wasn't as nice as Mike's.

Bobbi bumped Tina with her elbow. "I saw that."

"You pointed it out, hypocrite."

They arrived next to the blue sedan. Tina cleared her throat. "Everything all right?"

"His car won't start," Roslynn needlessly pointed out, glancing at Tina. "Can we give him a lift to the next exit? He called a tow truck two hours ago and it hasn't arrived yet."

The man in question straightened and met Tina's gaze. His blue eyes twinkled with humor, giving him a boyish appearance.

Tina guessed him to be about six-feet-four inches and approximately thirty-five to forty years old.

He ran his fingers through his sandy-blond hair, sending the silky locks standing on end. "I sure would appreciate a ride. I've been out here all morning. I'd like to get a hotel and something to eat."

Tina opened her mouth to decline when he abruptly extended his hand. "Name's Gary."

With no choice but to accept his show of greeting, Tina slid her palm against his. "Nice to meet you, Gary. But I don't pick up strangers."

"Tina!" Roslynn gasped, spinning around with her mouth hanging open. "It's not like he's out walking the interstate with his thumb out. His car broke down."

Fighting her inner common sense, Tina released his hand and nodded toward the car. "Where are you headed, Gary?"

"Home. I live in Tampa."

And then a thought struck her. "May I see the car's registration?"

"Sure." Stepping around Roslynn, Gary moved to the passenger side door, opened it, and then reached for the glovebox. He pulled a paper free and handed it to Tina.

Unfolding the paper, Tina read the name and address aloud. "Gary Rowland. 1417 County Highway 27. Tampa, Florida."

She handed him back the registration. "I'm sorry, Gary. It's not that I don't believe you, but without knowing you, I can't take the risk."

"May I speak with you a second?" Roslynn took hold of Tina's arm and guided her a few feet away. "Are you seriously just going to leave him out here in the heat? He showed you what you needed to see. I mean, look at him for God's sake. He's gorgeous. What are you afraid of?"

"Ted Bundy was gorgeous also, Roz. And you see how that turned out. He killed dozens of women."

Tina glanced at Gary once more. "I'm not saying he's dangerous, honey. I'm just not willing to take that chance."

Roz folded her arms over her chest. "You're being ridiculous. Where's your heart?"

"You have enough heart for the both of us," Tina shot back, instantly regretting it. Roslynn was one of her closest friends, and the pleading look in her eyes tore at Tina's heart.

"I'm sorry, Roz. I shouldn't have said that."

Roslynn gave her a lopsided smile. "So, we can give him a ride? He's awful cute."

Tina blew out a breath, her gaze once more straying to the man in question. "I don't feel good about this, Roz."

"I'll keep an eye on him," Roz assured her, her eyes lighting up. "He can sit in back with me."

Hoping she wouldn't live to regret it, Tina made a decision. "Fine. I'll take him as far as the Turnpike."

Roz's eyes lit up. "Thank you." She then spun around and hurried back to Gary's side.

Tina couldn't hear the exchange between the two. She strode to the SUV and climbed inside to find Bobbi already lounging in the passenger's seat and the engine running.

"She talked you into it, didn't she?"

Running a hand down her face, Tina met Bobbi's gaze. "Yep. And Mike would kill me if he knew."

"Then he won't know."

Tina glanced at her friend in time to see the twinkle in her eyes. "He'll know because we don't keep secrets from each other. I'll end up telling him."

"Whipped," Bobbi teased, showing a dimple in her cheek.

The back door opened presenting Roslynn and Gary, saving Tina from having to defend herself.

Truth was, Tina didn't keep things from Mike. She loved the honesty and trust they shared and hoped one day their relationship would go to the next level. Of course, that might never happen. Mike was terrified of marriage. And who could blame him. He'd had only his parents as an example.

"We're ready," Roslynn announced from her position behind Tina's seat.

Tina put the SUV in reverse, threw her arm over the seat to back out, and noticed a large, tan duffle bag resting on the floor next to Gary's legs.

He met her gaze, reached into his shirt pocket, and pulled out a twenty-dollar bill. "Thank you again for the lift."

Shaking her head, Tina attempted a cordial smile. "I appreciate the offer, Gary, but you can keep it."

"Are you sure?" he asked, still holding up the money.

Turning back to face the road, Tina nodded. "I'm positive."

Chapter Five

Tina turned up the radio enough to drown out the conversation taking place behind her. Roslynn and Gary seemed to have hit it off, if the blush on Roz's cheeks were any indication.

Tina had driven approximately fifty miles since leaving the rest stop, which meant that she would be approaching Interstate 75 pretty soon.

The sign came into view a moment later, indicating she had ten more miles before her turn-off.

Relaxing back against the seat, she fought a yawn, the soft love song playing on the radio lulling her into a comfortable state of sleepiness.

She reached for the knob, swiveling it slowly in search of something more upbeat, when an urgent-sounding news report caught her attention.

"The blue sedan was found at a rest area on Interstate 10, near mile marker 194 in Tallahassee. The body in the trunk is believed to belong to the owner of the car, although he hasn't been identified as of yet."

The news anchor continued to speak, but Tina was no longer listening. Her gaze had lifted to the rearview mirror to find Gary Rowland staring back at her, his hand wrapped in Roslynn's hair, and a pistol pressed against her cheek.

Tina's terrified gaze flicked to Roslynn only to find tears in her eyes—eyes that pleaded for help and…forgiveness.

"Turn it off," Gary demanded, nodding toward the radio.

Tina noticed her hand trembled as she switched off the news station. She didn't trust herself to speak, so she held her tongue.

Bobbi sat ramrod straight in her seat, her pale-as-a-sheet face visible in Tina's peripheral.

"We're in Lake City," the man in back rumbled. "Get off the interstate at the next exit."

Tina swallowed back her fear. "What do you want with us?"

He didn't answer, forcing Tina to glance in the mirror once more. What she saw there scared her more than the gun he held. His eyes, eyes so blue as to be appealing to most, held an evil in their depths that stole her breath.

And that evil was directed at her.

She directed her gaze back to the road, unable to look at him a second longer. But she could *feel* him, knew that he watched her.

Why had she allowed him into her vehicle? She should have listened to that voice in her head warning her to drive away and leave him at that rest area.

But she hadn't listened. She'd accepted him, taken him at his word. "Your name isn't Gary, is it?"

Why did she ask him such a thing? She didn't care about his name. But her brain seemed to be on autopilot, scrambling around, trying to make sense of her nightmare.

"Levi," he answered in a deep voice. "Gary was the owner of the sedan."

Unable to stop herself, she mumbled, "Is that who they found in the trunk?"

"It is."

Tina swallowed back the cry that rose in her throat. "Did you kill him?"

"Tina!" Bobbi hissed, wringing her hands from that passenger seat.

Levi laughed, a sinister sound that sent Tina's skin crawling. "He didn't deserve to live. Do you know that he cried the entire drive from Mississippi? No?" he prompted when Tina remained quiet. "You can't imagine what that was like for me. I rather enjoyed removing his tongue."

The sound that came from Roslynn was a mixture of terror and horror. She began to cry in earnest.

"Shut up!" Levi sneered, sending Roslynn into hysterics.

Tina knew if she didn't do something, and quick, Roslynn would end up like Gary.

Breathing through her own fear, Tina lifted her gaze to the mirror once more. The look on Roslynn's face ripped her heart in half.

Tina thought about her cell phone, resting in the slot beneath the radio. If she could get to it without being seen, she could dial 911. But from Levi's position in the back seat, she would never be able to pull it off without being seen. She needed to divert his attention. But how?

"Turn there at Calico Drive," Levi suddenly demanded, catching Tina off guard.

She took the road he'd indicated, noticing there were no houses in sight.

He then leaned forward, touching the side of Tina's face with that gun. "That dirt road up ahead. Take it."

Tina blinked back tears of panic. They were going to die. Of that, she had no doubt.

Chapter Six

Tina turned onto the dirt road, her foot riding the brake. Potholes lined the road, making driving difficult.

Nothing but trees could be seen in the distance. Not even a power pole indicating civilization ahead.

"Stop here," Levi snapped, tapping the side of her face once again.

Tina's leg shook so bad she had trouble stopping the vehicle.

She put it in park. "Please don't do this."

The sound of a zipper sent Tina's gaze back to the mirror. But Levi's head couldn't be seen. It took her a second to realize he was rifling through his duffle bag.

Roslynn's cries grew in volume until she became full-on hysterical.

Tears spilled from Tina's eyes. She turned in her seat in time to see Levi binding Roslynn's hands behind her back with duct tape. He then ripped off a piece and slapped it over her mouth.

"Much better," he announced in a singsong voice.

He straightened in his seat, his gaze going to the back of Bobbi's head. He tapped her on the shoulder as he'd done Tina. "You. What's your name?"

Bobbi made a panicked sound in the back of her throat. Tina could taste her friend's fear as surely as if it were her own. And it was.

"I asked you a question," Levi bit out.

"Leave her alone," Tina rushed out before she could stop herself.

Levi suddenly jumped out and yanked Bobbi's door open. He brought the gun to her head. "Name."

"Bobbi," Tina breathed, her stomach in her throat. "Her name's Bobbi!"

The corner of Levi's mouth lifted. "Now, that wasn't so hard, was it?"

He grabbed a handful of Bobbi's hair and jerked her out of the vehicle.

Bobbi began to beg, her words tearing a hole in Tina's chest.

Tina reached for her door handle, her mind screaming for her to run. But she couldn't. She wouldn't. Roslynn and Bobbi would be dead before she made it back to the road. *If* she made it.

"Don't even think about it," Levi growled, staring at Tina over Bobbi's head.

He slammed Bobbi face-first against the side of the SUV, yanked her arms behind her, and secured them with the duct tape. He then placed a piece over her mouth like he'd done with Roslynn.

Pulling Bobbi by the hair, he opened the door to the back row of seats and shoved her inside. He then slammed the door and got back in next to Roslynn.

"Give me the keys." Levi leaned forward, his arm extended, palm up.

Trembling, Tina pulled the keys free and dropped them onto his hand.

"Good girl," Levi praised. "Now, you sit there quietly. If you make a move, I'll blow Roslynn's brains all over the seats. Got it?"

Tina could only nod, too afraid to do anything else.

Roslynn began to scream behind the tape covering her mouth, the nightmarish sound filling the SUV with its horror.

The sound of material ripping could be heard over Roslynn's cries.

It took a second for Tina to realize what was happening behind her, and another for her to react.

She swung around in her seat, grabbing at the man tearing off Roslynn's clothes. "Stop it!"

He brandished the gun, aimed it at Tina's head, and pulled the hammer back. In a deadly soft voice, he said, "You die."

Tina froze, her eyes staring down the barrel of that gun. He was going to kill her. She knew it as surely as she knew none of them would make it out of there alive.

An image of Mike's smiling face floated through her mind. She would never see him again. Never have the chance to marry him, to grow old with him.

"Turn around in your seat," Levi bit out between clenched teeth. "And put your hands behind it."

Tina couldn't stop the tears from falling. She didn't cry for herself. No. She cried for Bobbi and Roslynn.

Facing forward, Tina slowly lowered her arms and presented that monster with her hands. Only, he didn't duct tape her as he'd done the others. He tied her wrists together with rope.

Tina stared straight ahead, unable to block out the sight of Levi in her mind's eye.

The jerky movements of his body coupled with the panicked sounds coming Roslynn confirmed Tina's worst fears. He was removing his pants.

Roslynn began to kick out with her legs, but she was no match for the man hovering above her.

She suddenly stopped fighting, a groan of despair slipping through the tape covering her mouth.

Tina's eyes slid shut, but she couldn't block out the sounds coming from that back seat. Nor could she stop the words Levi spoke from swimming through her head.

"Scream for me, Roslynn."

Chapter Seven

Mike Parker trailed through his father's home, his fingertips touching on everything in his path. The place felt like a tomb.

There were no pictures of Mike anywhere. Not even of his childhood.

That didn't surprise him. His father had been absent most of his life. The man had never even attended a ballgame...or his son's graduation.

Statues and paintings made up the living room, coupled with expensive furniture and rugs.

The kitchen was loaded with shelves of crystal and stainless-steel appliances and boasted a massive, cherrywood table. A table, Mike knew, had never seated a family.

Tina would love this house, Mike thought, moving down the hall to the master bedroom.

That was, if she agreed to marry him. And he intended to ask her when she returned from her trip to Orlando.

He dug out his cell phone, realizing that she should have arrived at her destination by now.

Scrolling through to find her name, he pressed it and brought the phone to his ear.

It rang at least five times and then went to voicemail. "Hey, you. I hope your trip was enjoyable. You're probably sleeping or out with your friends. Give me a call when you get this. I love you."

He ended the call.

It rang before he could replace it in his pocket. He recognized the number as one of the county phones.

"Parker," he answered, pressing the green key.

A female voice came over the line. "Mr. Parker? This is Karen Harvard, one of the animal control officers."

"Hey, Karen. What can I do for you?"

"We've got a situation out here on Piney Point Drive. I think you're familiar with the address."

Mike knew exactly the location she referred to. "I'm familiar. What's going on?"

"We got a call from a neighbor about a possible dog fight at the residence last night."

Anger filled Mike. "Did you notify Desiree Lenore? She's the investigator on call this weekend."

"I did. She's at the hospital, interviewing a shooting suspect."

Mike ran a hand through his hair. "Did the neighbor witness the fight?"

"No, sir. Not with the privacy fence up around the backyard. He heard it though."

"Okay, Karen. I'll meet you at the residence in ten minutes. I'm not far from there."

"Thank you, sir."

Ending the call, Mike strode through the house and out to his car. He started the engine and backed from the drive, attempting to call Tina once again.

Voicemail.

A strange feeling sifted through him. Tina had her phone with her at all times. Even in bed, she would wake to answer it. No matter what time it happened to be.

He stopped at the end of the driveway and sent her a text. *Missing you. Call me.*

He then phoned in to the station to let the sheriff know he would be taking the animal control call.

* * * *

Mike arrived at the address on Piney Point Drive approximately ten minutes later to find Karen, the animal control officer, standing out by her truck.

He pulled up next to her and rolled down his window. "Is anyone home that you know of?"

"Oh yeah," Karen answered, her eyes narrowing. "Sonny Jenkins has already made his appearance. Suffice it to say, he's not happy about us being here."

Mike nodded. "I'll handle it. You ready?"

She nodded. "As I'll ever be."

Rolling his window up, Mike pulled into Sonny Jenkins' drive. He didn't relish having to deal with Jenkins, but given the circumstances, he had little choice.

Sonny stepped from the house the moment Mike emerged from his car. "What's the problem, Investigator?"

Mike inwardly sighed. "You know exactly why I'm here, Mr. Perkins. We received a call that you were fighting dogs out here last night."

"I don't know which one of my nosey neighbors called you, but there ain't nothing going on here."

Mike crossed his arms over his chest. "Then you won't mind if I have a look around and see the dogs."

"You got a warrant?"

"Do I need one?" Mike shot back.

Sonny rested his hand on his hip. "If you think to search my property, then yeah, you do."

Mike knew there would be no use in arguing with the man. Because, well, frankly, Sonny was right. Mike *did* need a warrant.

Opening his car door, Mike slid behind the wheel. "I'll be back, Mr. Jenkins."

"I look forward to it."

Mike backed out, stopping next to the animal control truck. He lowered his window and met Karen's gaze. "He's not giving us permission to see the dogs. I'll have to get a warrant, and with it being the weekend, that won't be before Monday."

Karen's face reddened with anger. "Those dogs could be dead before then."

"I'm aware," Mike softly admitted, also hating to leave without the animals. But the law was the law, and if he went in there without that warrant, not only could he be sued, but the case wouldn't hold up in court. And the dogs would immediately be returned to Sonny Jenkins.

Pinching the bridge of his nose, Mike informed Karen that he would put in a call to the judge, in hopes of obtaining a warrant over the weekend. He neglected to tell her that a judge would never sign a warrant for possible dog fighting on the word of a neighbor who hadn't witnessed it.

Once Karen got into her truck, Mike continued on toward the stop sign. He picked up his phone and swiped his thumb across the screen. Tina had yet to call or respond to his text.

He tried her again.

Chapter Eight

Tina stared out the windshield of her SUV, unable to see through the tears spilling from her eyes. Roslynn had been assaulted. Not once but twice in the past three hours.

The screams coming from behind her taped mouth had long since stopped, and nothing could be heard but her painful, desolate-sounding moans.

Tina's cell phone had been vibrating off and on since her arrival on that dirt road. Though the display screen faced downward beneath the radio, she knew the caller was Mike. He would be checking to be sure she'd made it safely to Orlando. But she would never make it there. Of that, she had no doubt.

Levi suddenly leaned forward enough that Tina could see him in her peripheral. He pressed his nose against the side of her face. "You remind me of my ex-wife."

Tina shuddered, but kept her gaze straight ahead. She wouldn't give him the satisfaction of pulling away.

"Same color hair and eyes," he continued, sniffing at her neck. "You even have the same high cheekbones."

So, he'd been married before.

Tina locked her jaw when he ran his nose along its length. She wanted to turn and bite him, to scream in his face until the pain of what he'd done to Roslynn disappeared. But it would never disappear. Tina would relive it every time she closed her eyes for the rest of her life. Or until she died. Which she knew would be soon.

"Are you angry with me?" Levi asked, his voice a soft tone of mockery.

Tina clenched her teeth together to keep them from chattering, so great was her fear.

He reached around, cupped the other side of her head, and forced her to face him.

Tina closed her eyes, sending the hot tears swimming there spilling down her cheeks.

"Look at me, Tina."

She didn't want to look at him, for fear of finding her mortality lurking in his eyes.

He squeezed her jaw painfully. "I said. Look. At. Me."

Keeping her teeth locked together to prevent the chattering, Tina lifted her eyelids.

"That's better," Levi crooned, tilting his head to the side. "Why are you crying?"

Tina couldn't prevent the trembling in her body. She squeezed the seat with her bound arms, in hopes of calming the movement. It didn't work.

This monster, this insane psychopath, who held them all at gunpoint, who had unmercifully assaulted Roslynn for hours without ceasing, wanted to know why Tina cried?

She thought about trying to reason with him, but the insanity in his eyes assured her that it would do no good. She could beg him to let them go, but that wouldn't work either. He seemed to get off on the pleading sounds Roslynn made. And Tina knew deep down that he was searching for that same reaction from her as well. She wouldn't give it to him.

So, she said the first thing that came to mind. "My bladder hurts."

He stared back at her for long moments before letting go of her face. "Well, why didn't you say so?"

The feel of him freeing her wrists from the ropes nearly sent her crying out in relief. Her arms had long since gone to sleep, causing shooting pains to travel through her shoulders.

She brought her arms forward, rubbing at her aching wrists while glancing at her once again buzzing cell phone.

Levi jumped out, rounded the SUV, and opened her door. He leaned across her to snatch up the phone. "Someone's a very popular person. This thing's been buzzing for hours."

He swiped his thumb across the screen once the vibration ended. "Who is Mike Parker? He's called you six times."

"I said, who is Mike!" he snapped when Tina remained quiet.

Nerves shot through Tina's terrified body. She instinctively shielded her face with her hands, an unconscious move of protecting herself.

"A f-friend," she whispered, slowly lowering her hands. "He's a friend."

Levi studied her for several heartbeats before clicking on Mike's text message and scrolling through their private conversations. "Now, isn't that sweet. You two are obviously more than friends. Shall I read some of these texts aloud?"

Tina swallowed with difficulty. "He's my boyfriend."

Levi tucked some of her hair behind her ear. "Lies have always been second nature to women. Since the beginning of time."

He tossed the phone onto the ground behind him. "Get out."

Tina's body began to shake uncontrollably. Would he rape her if she got out of the vehicle?

He took the choice from her. Grabbing her by the arm, he yanked her toward him, sending her spilling out onto her side on the dirt road. "Do your business and be quick about it."

She scrambled up, terrified of him overpowering her. He expected her to relieve herself in front of him.

Tina knew better than to ask for privacy. It would likely get her killed.

Mortified beyond comprehension, she reached for the button on her jeans. Her hands shook to the point where it took several attempts to free the button and drag the zipper down.

With her face hot and terror riding her every move, she lowered her jeans and emptied her bladder.

Levi never took his gaze from her. He watched her beneath hooded eyelids, holding that gun in her direction.

Once finished, she quickly straightened and pulled up her pants. But Levi didn't move.

Tina could hear Roslynn and Bobbi crying inside the SUV. She wanted to run to Roslynn, to comfort her, to hold her close.

"Get in," Levi demanded in that eerily soft voice that made Tina's skin crawl.

She had to squeeze between him and the vehicle to get back inside.

His arm snaked out, stopping her from slipping by him.

He leaned down and covered her mouth with his.

Nausea was instant, quickly replacing her fear. Bile rushed to her throat, taking her breath.

Tina held completely still, too afraid to move. But she could no more stop the gag reflex than she could prevent the sun from rising in the mornings.

Levi laughed, pulling back enough to look into her eyes. "I can taste your beautiful fear."

She didn't respond, only stared up at a place beyond his shoulder.

And then he stepped back, waving that gun toward the door. "Go on."

Tina backed inside the vehicle, unable to turn her back on the monster standing so close.

Once her legs were clear, he shut the door, rounded the SUV, and climbed inside.

Dropping the keys over her shoulder, he demanded, "Start the engine."

Tina grabbed up the keys with shaky fingers. It took three attempts to insert the correct one into the ignition, but she somehow managed.

The engine roared to life, and with it, the air conditioning. Cool air blasted her overheated face to dry the tears lingering on her cheeks.

"Hands behind the seat," Levi demanded, sending Tina's already nauseated stomach into vomit mode.

She slowly extended her arms behind her, her eyes sliding closed when he tied her wrists with that rope.

Roslynn's hoarse, muffled screams soon filled the SUV's interior once more, sending Tina into full-blown panic mode.

She jerked at her bonds, to no avail. "Ah, God, leave her alone. Please!"

Levi only laughed.

"I'm begging you," Tina cried, attempting to see him over her shoulder. "Take me instead! Please, just take me!"

Her pleas fell on deaf ears.

Roslynn's screams grew more frantic, changing from terror to something deeper, something far darker. Tina recognized it as agony.

Something wet suddenly sprayed the side of Tina's face. It took her a second to realize it was blood and another for her mind to completely snap.

Tina's teeth began to chatter, and her pleading, tormented words blended together to form a haunting chant she herself didn't understand.

Bobbi's muffled screams soon bled over into Tina's mind, telling her without words that Bobbi witnessed what was happening to Roslynn.

Tina couldn't think past the sounds coming from behind her. Levi was torturing Roslynn in ways that her brain couldn't process.

The moans abruptly stopped. The back door opened, and the sound of something heavy dropping to the ground reached Tina's ears. Levi had shoved Roslynn from the vehicle.

Unable to stop herself, Tina slowly turned her head toward the driver's side window. She strained against the ropes, leaning over as far as her bonds would allow. There, lying on that dirt road, was Roslynn's nude form.

Tina stared in disbelief as spots danced before her eyes.

Blood covered most of Roslynn's body. Her throat had been cut, and dozens of stab wounds bled freely from her torso.

"Roslynnnnnnnnnn!" Tina cried, her mind rejecting what her heart knew to be true. Roslynn was dead.

Tina vomited.

Chapter Nine

Mike left the sheriff's office after being denied the warrant to search Sonny Jenkins' place. He wasn't so much denied as put off until Monday.

Putting a call in to Karen, Mike broke the news he knew she wouldn't want to hear. He himself hadn't wanted to hear it. And Karen was even more passionate about animals than Mike was. If that were possible.

"Please tell me you got the warrant," Karen blurted upon answering.

Mike exhaled a frustrated breath. "The judge wouldn't sign it. It'll be Monday before we can get one."

"Monday will be too late," Karen practically growled. "Jenkins will have moved the dogs by then and cleaned everything up."

"I know, Karen. Trust me, I know. But it's out of my hands. I tried. I really did."

Karen sighed through the line. "I'm sorry. It just irks me to no end to imagine those poor dogs suffering at the hands of that creep."

"It does me too. I'm off on Monday, but I'll let Desiree know the situation. She'll obtain the warrant first thing Monday morning. It's the best that I can do."

Mike ended the call, his heart heavy with the knowledge that no arrest would be made that day, and those dogs would likely be moved before he could save them.

He then called Desiree and filled her in on everything that had gone on. She assured him that she would handle it as soon as she had the warrant to search Jenkins' property in hand.

Climbing behind the wheel of his car, Mike started the engine and glanced at his watch. It had been another two hours since he'd last left Tina a message.

He scrolled through his phone to be sure he hadn't missed a text from her. Nothing.

Worried, he tried her cell phone again. Straight to voicemail. Something was wrong. He'd been an investigator long enough to sense trouble.

Pulling up the internet on his phone, Mike typed in the name of the hotel in Orlando where he and Tina had made reservations.

Locating the number, he clicked on it. It immediately began to ring.

"Dolphin Inn," a feminine voice announced.

"Hi. This is Mike Parker. Tina Duggar and I had reservations today at noon. Room 302. I wasn't able to make it, but Tina should have arrived a few hours ago. Can you put me through to the room?"

"Hold please." There was a brief pause. "Miss Duggar hasn't checked in yet."

Warning bells went off in Mike's head. "Are you sure? She was supposed to be there hours ago."

"I'll check again."

Mike could hear the woman's fingers clicking on a keyboard.

"I'm sorry, sir. But no one has checked into that room."

"Thank you." Mike pressed the end key and dialed Tina's cell once more. Voicemail.

Running a hand down his face, he drove out of the parking lot, his stomach in knots. Where could she be?

Mike understood that Bobbi and Roslynn were with her, and the three of them could have stopped at a flea market or something along the way. But if that were the case, Tina would have answered his call or returned his text by now.

And then a thought occurred to him. Tina and he both had iPhones, which meant that as long as her Find My Phone app was on, he should be able to locate her cell phone. Especially since she'd given him her sign in information.

He pulled off the side of the road, opened the app, and signed into Tina's account. He then clicked on the green dot indicating her phone. It took a minute for the GPS to ping her location. She was somewhere off Calico Drive in Lake City, which was the halfway mark between the Panhandle and Orlando.

His heart began to pound.

Closing the app, Mike pulled into traffic and drove like a bat out of Hell to Bobbi's house. He didn't have her cell phone number, but her husband, Joey, would.

It took Mike ten minutes to reach Bobbi Deloach's place. A black truck sat in the drive next to a small, white hatchback.

Mike parked behind the truck and got out.

"Can I help you?" a deep voice called out from the side yard.

Mike turned and strode in the man's direction to find him watering some plants. "Joey Deloach?"

"Yes." He released the trigger on the hose's nozzle. "Who's asking?"

Mike extended his hand. "Name's Mike Parker. I'm a friend of Tina Duggar's."

Joey accepted Mike's outstretched palm. "What can I do for you?"

Releasing Joey's hand, Mike got right to the point. "I'm assuming that your wife went to Orlando with Tina."

Joey nodded, laying down the hose. "She and Roslynn Earnhardt both did. Is something wrong?"

Mike hesitated. On the one hand, he didn't want to upset the man if the women were simply shopping in Lake City, and Tina had left her phone in the vehicle. But his gut was telling him otherwise.

"I'm not sure. I've been calling and texting Tina for hours, with no answer. I called the hotel where they were supposed to be, but the woman at the front desk said they hadn't checked in yet. Have you heard from your wife?"

Joey wiped the sweat from his forehead and pulled his cell phone from a clip on the side of his belt. "No, I haven't. But that's not surprising. She's in one of her moods at the moment."

Mike watched Joey swipe the phone's screen, obviously checking for messages. "I did a search of Tina's phone on an app we share, and it showed her in Lake City. That's a good three hours from Orlando."

Joey pressed a button on his cell phone and lifted it to his ear. He then lowered it. "It went straight to voicemail. You don't think something happened to them, do you?"

Mike pulled a business card from his shirt pocket and handed it to Joey. "I'm sure they're fine. Let me know if you hear from your wife."

"Will do. I'll shoot you a text, so you'll have my number. If Tina contacts you, give me a holler."

With a nod, Mike returned to his car.

Once he had the engine running, he opened the app on his cell once again. The flashing green light representing Tina's phone remained at the same place it was before. Near Calico Drive in Lake City, Florida.

Making a decision, Mike backed out of the Deloach's drive and headed toward home. He would pack a bag and head south. Something was definitely wrong.

Chapter Ten

Tina drove slowly up Calico Drive, her mind numb from shock and disbelief. The psycho sitting behind her had tortured and killed Roslynn.

He had dumped her from the vehicle like a bag of garbage to bleed out on the cold dirt covered earth she lay on.

Tina had been forced to use Roslynn's bloody clothes to clean up her own vomit.

I'm having a nightmare, Tina's mind screamed; she was still unable to take a deep breath. *I'm going to wake up any minute now and find myself in bed at the hotel.*

But she knew that to be a lie the moment she thought it.

Bobbi still cried from the third-row seat. Tina could hear her over her own labored breathing.

Levi suddenly leaned forward and snatched up Roslynn's purse. He dug around inside, pulling her cell phone free. He then tossed it out the window.

"Where's the other one's phone?"

Tina knew he spoke to her. He wouldn't have questioned Bobbi with her mouth taped shut.

"I don't know."

He grabbed a handful of Tina's hair and yanked her head back against the seat. Hard.

She cried out in pain. "I swear I don't know!"

He released her, and the sounds of him rummaging through bags filled the SUV. "Ah, here it is." He tossed out that phone as well.

There would be no way for them to be tracked now. Tina's 2001 SUV hadn't been designed with a GPS system installed.

When Levi ended up killing Bobbi and her, their bodies would probably never be found.

And he would kill them.

And then a thought struck Tina. Her cell phone had a phone finder app on it. But she couldn't remember if she'd left it on or not. She prayed to God she had, so Mike would be able to locate it. At least they would find Roslynn's body.

Roslynn... Tina's heart hurt worse than she ever imagined it could. The pain of Roslynn's death far overshadowed her own fear of dying.

Levi climbed over the console and plopped down in the passenger seat. "I'm hungry. Are you hungry, Tina?"

Tina didn't look at him, though she could see him in her peripheral. He had put on his seatbelt.

"I asked you a question, Tina."

Swallowing back her terror, she shook her head.

"Pity. Once we hit the main highway up ahead, I want you to pull into the drive-thru of the first fast food place we come to. I need to eat."

How could he think about eating after what he'd just done? Tina's stomach had been churning nonstop since she'd retched back on that dirt road.

Levi grew quiet for a moment, and then, "Tell me about Mike."

Tina didn't want to speak of Mike to this monster. She couldn't bring herself to speak to him, period. Let alone about Mike.

"If you can't find it in your heart to talk, perhaps I should remove your tongue. Seems to me, you don't need it anyhow."

Her heart lurched. She fought tears of anger and fear, opened her mouth, closed it, and then tried again. "What do you want to know?"

Was that her voice sounding strong and clear? Maybe if she could keep him talking, it would give her time to think of a way to escape. But with Bobbi being bound up in the back of the SUV, Tina couldn't imagine how she would pull that off.

"What kind of work does he do?" Levi asked, gazing in Tina's direction.

She wasn't about to admit that Mike was an investigator with the sheriff's department. That would likely set the lunatic off. "He does construction."

"Like building houses?"

Tina's stomach tightened. Was he baiting her? "No. He hangs sheetrock."

"Ah," Levi murmured softly. "Funny, you don't strike me as the type to be with a construction worker."

Tina wondered what he meant by that remark. Her father had hung sheetrock for a living. Which was why she'd chosen that particular lie over any other. If Levi had questioned her further, she would have been able to answer without hesitation.

"How long have you been seeing him?"

"Three years." That part wasn't a lie.

She could see Levi studying her, but she kept her gaze on the road.

He opened the glovebox and began sifting through it. "How did you meet?"

Tina chanced a look in the rearview mirror to find Bobbi sitting up, her terrified gaze locked on Tina's.

"I hired him to do some work for me," Tina answered, sending Bobbi a look that she hoped conveyed she would do everything she could to get them out of there.

Levi paused in his plundering. "You've been together for three years. Any kids?"

"No kids."

"And what is it that you do for a living, Tina?"

She sent Bobbi one last determined look and then focused on the questions being asked by Levi. "I work with animal control."

He lifted his head. "You're far too prissy to be out chasing down rabid dogs."

Tina wanted to point out that there was nothing prissy about her, but she held her tongue. "I'm not an animal control officer. I work in dispatch," she hedged.

Flipping the glovebox closed, he reached across the seat and took hold of her hand. "You're trembling."

Of course she was trembling. She was petrified of the psycho sitting next to her. Especially after seeing what he'd done to Roslynn.

His thumb began to slide across her knuckles, prompting the return of her nausea.

The blessed glimpse of giant golden arches came into sight, nearly doubling Tina over in relief. Surely to God, she would be able to get someone's attention while they were there.

She pulled the SUV into the drive-thru line, easing up to stop mere inches behind the car in front of her.

Levi unbuckled his seatbelt, climbed into the back with Bobbie, and pushed her down, out of sight.

He called up front to Tina, "This pistol is aimed at your friend's head. One wrong move on your part, one suspicious word, and she dies. Understood?"

"Yes," Tina whispered, panicked that Levi was now back there with Bobbi.

Tina could imagine how terrified Bobbi must be.

Levi informed Tina of what he wanted to eat, ending with, "I'm watching you in the side mirror. No eye contact. Move slowly and speak clearly."

Pulling her wallet from her purse, Tina eyed the debit card resting there. Mike would know to trace her card usage once he realized she was missing. *When* he realized it. And she prayed it wouldn't be too late when he did.

She tugged the card free...

Chapter Eleven

Mike packed a couple of shirts and two pairs of jeans into a duffle bag, along with underwear and socks.

He added some ammunition for his Glock and tucked a knife and few bottles of water inside.

He'd notified the sheriff's department in Lake County of his findings in an attempt to get a jump on locating Tina. But all he had was a GPS location of her cell phone pinging off Calico Drive.

What if she knew someone on that road and was visiting or currently sleeping at their place? She would be highly upset if the sheriff's department showed up there and embarrassed her.

Mike hesitated for a second, but then pushed the thought aside. In the three years he'd known her, Tina had never not replied to his texts, let alone neglected to answer his calls.

Not to mention, Bobbi wasn't answering her husband either.

Neither Joey nor Mike had Roslynn's number, and Mike had no idea if she had family in the area. The only thing he knew about Roslynn was that she happened to be a traveling nurse.

He put in a call to the Bay County Sheriff's Department.

Someone picked up on the second ring. "Bay Count EOC, this is Mandy."

"Mandy? This is Mike Parker." Mike went through the details of everything that had happened since Tina's departure that morning. "Mr. Deloach hasn't been able to reach his wife either. Will you see what you can find on Roslynn Earnhardt?"

"I'll get back to you with my findings," Mandy assured him before hanging up the phone.

Mike grabbed his bag, locked up his house, and hurried out to his car. He had a three-hour drive ahead of him to reach Lake City. He only prayed that he would find Tina there.

His cell rang about twenty minutes into the drive. He snatched it up. "Parker."

"Mr. Parker, it's Mandy. I have some information on Roslynn Earnhardt. Apparently, we sent a deputy out last year to her last known address." She rattled off the address along with a phone number. "That's all I could find."

"Thank you, Mandy. That was a huge help."

Ending the call, Mike dialed the cell number the dispatcher had given him. Voicemail. *"You've reached Roslynn. You know what to do."*

Grinding his teeth in frustration, Mike pushed the end button, laid the phone down on the console, and pressed the gas a bit harder.

* * * *

An hour into the drive to Lake City, Mike received a call from the sheriff there. "Parker? This is Sheriff Wilcox. We spoke earlier."

"Hi, Sheriff. I appreciate your help. Did you find the girls?"

The sheriff hesitated. "We located the cell phone... And a body."

Mike's entire world spun on its axis. His mind couldn't comprehend the sheriff's words. He swallowed several times in an attempt to speak.

"Mr. Parker?"

"I'm here," Mike managed to get out. "Was it...Tina Duggar?"

A brief pause ensued. "There was no identification on the body."

Mike drove faster. "I'll be there in two hours."

The sheriff gave Mike the location of the body. "We'll be here for a while, collecting evidence."

"I'll see you then."

Mike ended the call, his jaw clenched in agony. Tina couldn't be dead. He refused to believe it.

Chapter Twelve

Tina drove in silence, acutely aware of the maniac seated next to her. She could hear Bobbi softly crying in the third-row seat and wondered how much pain she was in. The fact that Bobbi's arms had been secured behind her back for hours assured Tina that she must be in agony.

She chanced a look in the rearview mirror but was unable to see Bobbi's face. "Can we remove her tape for minute?"

Levi swiveled his head in Tina's direction. "What for?"

"She's in pain," Tina responded as calmly as she could manage. The last thing she wanted was to set Levi off.

He stared back at her for what felt like an eternity, sending nerves scattering throughout her body.

"She's not in as much pain as she will be."

Gut-wrenching terror slid through Tina. "Please don't hurt her. I'm begging you."

"Begging doesn't become you, Tina."

And it didn't. Tina had never been the type to beg for anything, but she would bow down and lick the soles of this psycho's shoes, if it meant he wouldn't harm Bobbi. "Then I'm asking you."

He had the audacity to chuckle. "You're *asking* me? As if that somehow gives you the power to change the outcome."

Bobbi's crying grew in volume.

Tina stared at the road, noticing that they were approaching Marianna. So close to home, yet it might as well be a thousand miles away.

"Get off the interstate at the next exit," Levi demanded, sending Tina's already frazzled nerves into orbit.

"You don't have to do this," Tina rushed out, hoping her words would reach a part of him that harbored some humanity. "You can let Bobbi go. You don't need her. You have me."

He reached over and laid his disgusting palm on Tina's thigh. "You're right. I don't need her. Now take the exit or I'll kill you both." He pointed the gun in Tina's direction.

With no other choice, Tina took the offramp he'd indicated. It happened to be an exit that consisted of two gas stations and a peanut stand. Very few people were in sight.

Levi lifted the gun higher. "Go right at the stop sign."

Tina took a right. She or Bobbi would die when they reached their destination. She could hear it in Levi's voice.

After she drove for approximately a mile, Levi directed her to another clay road that would lead them to God knew where.

Tears were already falling from Tina's eyes. Panic had set in to the point where she had trouble pressing the gas.

About two miles into the drive down the clay road, Levi ordered Tina to stop the vehicle.

He climbed out, rounded the SUV, and opened the door directly behind her. "Arms behind your back."

"Oh God, please don't do this!" Tina cried, placing her arms behind her seat. "Why can't you just take me? You don't need to do this!"

He secured her wrists with the rope and then slapped some duct tape over her mouth. "There. I'm sick to death of your whining."

The sound of the third door opened, and Bobbi's muffled screams filled Tina's head.

Tina instinctively fought against her bonds, somewhere deep in her mind hoping to break free. Even though she knew it to be impossible. But panic prompted irrational thinking, and

Tina had blown way past panic the second they'd turned onto that clay road.

Levi suddenly appeared next to Tina's window, holding a terrified Bobbi against his body.

He smiled at Tina, a look that promised a nightmare to come.

Dragging Bobbi around to the front of the SUV, Levi threw her onto the ground.

She landed face-first in the clay.

Tina could barely see through her tears as she struggled with the ropes binding her. The tape covering her mouth prevented her screams from being heard, which was what Levi intended.

Bobbi's screams were muffled by the tape as well, but the frantic movements of her body said it all. She managed to roll to her back, her horror-filled gaze locked on Tina. She pleaded with her eyes for Tina to help her, an image that

Tina would never be able to unsee... An image that would follow her to the grave.

Tina wanted to close her eyes, to block out the scene unfolding in front of her. But she couldn't. She looked on in horror as Levi cut the clothes from Bobbi's body.

He laughed at her struggles, her cries, and then ripped the tape free from her mouth.

"My baby!" Bobbi cried, staring up at him through her tears. "Please don't hurt my baby!"

Levi stilled. He didn't speak or move for several minutes, simply watched Bobbi through the haze of his insanity.

And just as quickly as he'd snapped, he calmly closed the knife he held, tucked it into his back pocket, and strode back to the passenger side of the SUV.

Once inside, he sat there without moving, his gaze locked on a naked Bobbi, lying on her back on that clay road.

Just as Tina thought he would climb out and return to his torture, he leaned over the seat, untied her hands, and then ripped the tape from her mouth. "Drive."

Tina didn't hesitate. She would get that monster as far away from Bobbi as she possibly could.

Chapter Thirteen

Mike wasn't sure how long he'd been driving. His mind had gone numb the second the sheriff had told him about the body they'd found.

Why had he let Tina go on this trip without him? He should have insisted she wait for him, or better yet, he should have put his own business on hold until they returned.

So what if the attorney would be gone for two months? Mike didn't give a crap about his father's will, any more than he gave a crap about his father.

The man had never been there for him. Never. But Tina had. And now, she was probably lying on the side of the road, dead, because he hadn't put her first.

A groan rose up in Mike's throat. He released it into the interior of his car in an effort to relieve some of the pain gripping his chest. But it only intensified.

The GPS on his phone prompted him to take the next left. He was nearly at his destination.

Arriving on Calico Drive, Mike caught sight of three patrol cars up ahead. He pulled alongside the road and got out.

One of the deputies approached. "This is a crime scene."

Mike flashed his badge. "I'm aware. Sheriff Wilcox is expecting me."

The deputy nodded. "Come with me."

Mike walked along next to the deputy down a winding dirt road. He had a thousand questions he wanted to ask, but somehow, he managed to restrain himself. He knew the deputy wouldn't have the answers he sought.

The two of them eventually rounded a curve, and the crime scene came into view. The area had been taped off, and the usual investigative paraphernalia littered the area.

A tall, older man trailed over, his hand extended. "Parker?"

Mike nodded, accepting the man's palm. But he barely met the man's gaze, his own attention drawn to the tarp-covered body up ahead.

"I need to see," Mike informed Wilcox without taking his gaze from that tarp.

The sheriff lifted the yellow tape. "Be advised. It's bad."

Mike's stomach lurched. His heart pounded hard enough he was sure the sheriff could hear it. If Tina lay under that covering… He couldn't finish the thought.

The two of them walked around the evidence markers to approach the body from behind.

Mike locked his teeth together, lowered to his haunches, and hesitated.

"Take your time," the sheriff softly offered. "I'll just give you a minute." He moved back several feet.

Gathered every ounce of courage he had in him, Mike took a deep breath and carefully tugged the material back.

Relief was swift, nearly doubling him over with the power of it. The milky-colored eyes staring blankly at the sky didn't belong to his beloved Tina.

"Roslynn," Mike whispered, his heart aching for the young woman. "I'm so sorry."

He peeled the tarp farther back, his gaze touching on the dozens of stab wounds lining her torso and stomach. She'd been stabbed to death.

Covering the body once more, Mike pushed to his feet and faced the sheriff. "Was she raped?"

The sheriff nodded. "That can't be officially determined without an autopsy, but the signs are there."

Mike's stomach rolled. "Her name is Roslynn Earnhardt. She was traveling to Orlando with Tina. Along with another friend named Bobbi Deloach."

"Sir?" Another deputy came jogging over, careful to stay behind the tape. "We've found two more cell phones."

Disappointment was swift. Mike didn't have to ask to know the phones belonged to Bobbi and Roslynn. "There will be no other way to track Tina without those phones. Her SUV has no GPS installed."

"Does she have credit cards or a debit card?" the sheriff asked.

Mike nodded. "She has a debit card for sure. I've seen her use it."

Lifting the tape, the sheriff offered, "Follow me to the station. We'll run a trace on her debit card. With any luck, we'll get a hit."

A tiny spark of hope welled to life inside Mike. Though whomever had Tina and Bobbi knew enough to dump their phones. Which meant he would likely know to get rid of the debit cards as well. Mike prayed not.

Chapter Fourteen

Tina drove back to the interstate, grateful beyond words that Levi had left Bobbi alive. She wondered if Bobbi's cry for her unborn child had been the reason for the psycho's mercy.

Bobbi is pregnant, Tina thought for the hundredth time. She'd come so close to losing her life and the life of her unborn baby. But she'd lived. *Thank God, she lived.*

"A penny for your thoughts," Levi muttered in that singsong voice that made Tina's skin crawl.

She wouldn't mention Bobbi's name for fear that he'd make her turn the SUV around and go back to finish what he'd started.

Bobbi was not only naked, but her hands were taped behind her back. Tina wouldn't risk it.

Instead, she murmured, "I'm hungry."

If she could get back to a drive-thru somewhere, she could use her debit card again to let Mike know which direction she was headed. She only prayed he had figured out that she hadn't made it to the hotel.

"You should have eaten back in Lake City," Levi returned, his voice an unfeeling, monotone rasp of insanity.

Tina pushed back her fear. "I wasn't hungry then. Especially after seeing what you'd done to Roslynn."

"She was a whore who deserved what she got."

Tina's face grew hot with anger, but she kept that particular emotion in check. "She wasn't a whore. She was just misunderstood."

"She jumped all over the opportunity to give me a ride. I saw the lust in her eyes."

That doesn't make her a whore, Tina wanted to scream, but she remained quiet.

"Pull off at the next exit."

Suddenly terrified again, Tina slowed at the offramp and coasted to the upcoming stop sign. She waited there for instructions on what to do next.

Levi waved the gun toward the windshield. "You wanted food. Get it and be quick about it."

Relieved, Tina spotted a drive-thru. She flipped on her blinker, looked both ways, and turned left. "I also need to use the bathroom."

"You're fortunate I'm allowing you to eat. Shut your mouth and drive."

She had gone too far. She could hear the anger in his voice.

Desperate to keep him from snapping, Tina whispered, "I'm sorry."

She pulled into the drive-thru and placed her order around a throat gone dry. Her thoughts were on everything but food. She wondered how long before he forced her into the woods and stabbed her to death like he'd done Roslynn.

Roslynn… She was really gone, her life cruelly taken from her by the sadistic monster parked in Tina's passenger seat.

Tina's heart ached more than she ever imagined it could. Her body felt hollow, and her head throbbed to the beat of her heart.

With her order placed, she pulled up to the window, reached for her wallet, and pulled a debit card free.

Levi's fingers were suddenly around her wrist. "Cash. You pay with cash."

Disappointment was instant. If she couldn't use her card, Mike would never be able to trace her location.

With no other choice, she dug out the appropriate amount and passed it through the now open drive-thru window.

The woman handed Tina her change and then her bag of food. She then held out the drink, which Tina accepted without looking at her.

Rolling up her window, Tina drove away from the restaurant.

Levi took a sip of Tina's soda and then opened her bag of food. He peeled the wrapper away from the burger, holding it up for her to take a bite. "Open."

Tina couldn't possibly put that burger in her mouth. She would vomit in her lap. Her stomach had been rolling nonstop since Roslynn's death.

"I said open."

Left with no choice, Tina forced her teeth apart and took a small bite.

Her jaws watered with the need to retch, but she somehow managed to swallow without gagging.

He handed her a French fry, which she took between numb fingers. "Why are you doing this?"

"I really don't want to kill you right now, Tina. I'm rather enjoying your company. But if you keep running that mouth, you'll find yourself in a ditch somewhere."

He'd said, *right now*. Which meant that he was merely prolonging her death.

She pushed that French fry into her mouth, choking it down without chewing. And on it went with Tina eating without tasting it. The food had become something to fill the silence, the void, while she attempted to figure out a way of escaping him.

Chapter Fifteen

"Tina Duggar's debit card was used four hours ago at a fast food restaurant not far from here," Sheriff Wilcox informed a pacing Mike, giving him the name of the eatery.

Mike slowed his pacing. "Is that it?"

The sheriff shook his head. "No. There were a couple more transactions earlier for gas and such. But this is the only one in close proximity to the crime scene. I've issued a BOLO on Miss Duggar's SUV."

Mike headed toward the door, speaking over his shoulder as he went. "Which direction is the restaurant?"

"I'll show you." The sheriff grabbed his hat and left the station behind Mike. "Follow me."

Jogging over to his car, Mike slid behind the wheel, started the engine, and sped out of the parking lot, practically on the sheriff's bumper.

A few minutes later, Mike strode past the golden arches and into the fast food joint in search of the manager.

A short, middle-aged woman approached. "May I help you?"

"My name is Mike Parker. I'm an investigator with the Bay County Sheriff's Department in Panama City Beach. Are you the manager on duty?"

The woman nodded, a small indention appearing between her eyes. "Name's Malina. Is everything all right?"

Mike retrieved his wallet from his back pocket and pulled a picture of Tina from its depths. He presented it to Malina. "Do you recognize this woman?"

Malina accepted the photo, stared it briefly, and then handed it back. "I'm sorry. She doesn't look familiar."

"Look again." Mike held it up for her to see. "She would have been here approximately four hours ago. Maybe with a man and at least one other woman."

Malina shook her head. "I've been here for about seven hours. But that doesn't mean anything. There are hundreds of people that come in here on a daily basis. Maybe they used the drive-thru."

That got Mike's attention. "Who was working the drive-thru around that time?"

"Kayla," the manager called out, flagging a tallish, dark-haired girl over.

Mike presented Kayla with the picture of Tina. "Do you recall seeing this woman in the drive-thru about four hours ago?"

Kayla gazed at the photo. "Yeah. I remember her because it looked like she'd been crying."

"Was anyone else with her?" Mike questioned, attempting to keep his demeanor calm.

Kayla nodded. "Yes. I didn't get a good look at him, but I remember wondering if the two of them had been arguing."

"Think carefully, Kayla. It's extremely important."

Her eyes suddenly lit up. "His hand was on her arm, holding onto her possessively. He had letters tattooed on his thumb and the rest of his fingers. I assumed it was her name."

Mike's heart skipped a beat. "What was the name?"

"Renee."

"Is there anything else you can tell me about the man?"

Kayla appeared thoughtful. "Like I said, I didn't get a good look at him, but I do remember he had sandy-blond hair."

"What about the vehicle they were in?"

"Some sort of large SUV, I think. A black one."

Mike could hear the sheriff questioning the manager about a possible security feed.

"Thank you, Kayla," Mike murmured, returning the picture of Tina to his wallet.

He faced Malina and the sheriff in time to hear the manager state that the security camera at the drive-thru no longer worked.

Mike left the restaurant with the sheriff in tow. "Renee. The name on his hand was Renee."

Wilcox rounded his patrol car. "I'll run it through and see if we have anyone in our database with that particular marking. It's a long shot but worth a try."

"How did this psychopath end up in Tina's SUV?" Mike wondered aloud.

The sheriff squinted against the setting sun. "Maybe she picked him up."

Mike opened his mouth to argue that Tina would never allow a hitchhiker into her vehicle, when the look on the sheriff's face stopped him.

"What are you thinking?"

The sheriff ran his fingers along his jaw. "FHP found a blue sedan at a rest area not far from here."

Mike waited quietly for Wilcox to make his point.

"They found a body in the trunk. He'd been murdered."

The knot in Mike's stomach grew to the point where he feared he'd be sick. "Let's go."

Chapter Sixteen

Tina had been driving for approximately thirty minutes when Levi waved the gun in her direction. "Get off right here."

She didn't speak, only turned off at the exit he'd indicated.

"That gas station, there," he pointed out, nodding toward a small convenience store up ahead.

Tina's heart began to thump heavily in her chest. There were two cars parked along the side of the store. If she could get someone's attention, she might have a chance of getting away.

"Pull up next to that green car over there."

She did as he ordered, parking on the right side of a medium-sized green four-door.

A woman came around the corner, wearing white shorts and a pink tank top, her red hair pulled back into a ponytail.

She stopped at the driver's side door of her car, her head lowered while she dug through her handbag.

Tina assumed she hunted for her keys.

"Get your purse and follow me." Levi opened his door and got out, his duffle bag in hand.

Tina did as he said, watching him attempt to hide the gun behind the duffle bag.

He slowly approached the woman, with Tina at his side.

Tina watched in horror as he slipped up behind the redhead, pressed the barrel of the gun against her back, and murmured something low that Tina couldn't hear.

The woman stiffened, her face growing pale. She unlocked her car door with trembling fingers and slid behind the wheel.

Tears were present in the woman's eyes, but she didn't call out for help. Not that Tina blamed her. With the gun aimed at her, the woman had no choice but to do as Levi said, or die there in that store parking lot.

Levi opened the back door and then ordered Tina to get up front with the terrified woman.

"Drive," he demanded of the woman the second Tina pulled her door closed.

Tears began leaking from the redhead's eyes. She drove away from the store, stopping at the main road. "W-what do you want with me?"

"Give me her purse," Levi demanded of Tina.

Tina couldn't bring herself to continue looking at the driver. The fear and anxiety on the woman's face were too much to bear.

Tina grabbed onto the woman's purse and passed it over the seat to Levi.

Long moments passed before Levi spoke. "Leslie Gilmore. That's a nice name. Take a left to the interstate, Leslie. And then head east."

"P-please," Leslie whispered, her voice dripping with terror. "Take the car, the money in my bag, just please let me go."

The barrel of that gun was suddenly pressed against the back of Leslie's head. "If you don't want to die right now, get this car on the road."

Tina turned to stare out her window, unable to stomach the sobbing sounds the woman made. She knew it would do Leslie no good to cry and beg. The monster in that back seat lacked empathy of any kind.

Except with Bobbi, Tina thought, watching the trees along the side of the road go past. He had allowed Bobbi to live. *Because of her unborn baby.*

Something inside Levi had stopped him from killing a woman with child. A psychopath wouldn't have felt the empathy required to do the right thing. Yet, Levi had. *But why?*

If Tina could somehow get inside his head, maybe she could reach him, reach the part he'd shown when confronted with Bobbi's pregnancy.

Scared beyond words, Tina rubbed her sweaty palms along the front of her jeans. This is it, she silently chanted, turning in her seat to face the monster. But the look in his eyes prevented her from speaking.

Pure, unadulterated evil stared back at her from his glittering blue orbs.

She quickly straightened, shifting her gaze back to the windshield, unable to do anything but listen to Levi instruct Leslie on where to turn next.

Tina wasn't sure how long Leslie drove, when the car stopped on what looked to be an abandoned road.

"Get out," Levi barked, tossing Leslie's cell phone out the window.

Tina instinctively knew that this would be the end of the line for the terrified redhead.

Waving the gun between them, Levi demanded again, "Get out."

Tina quickly exited the car, as did Leslie.

Leslie had cried so much that mascara streaked down her cheeks. The sheer terror in her eyes was enough to haunt the Devil himself.

Levi appeared next to them, tape and rope in one hand and the gun in the other. "Turn around and put your hands on the car. Both of you."

This is it, Tina realized, placing her palms against the vehicle. *This is where we die.*

Levi secured Leslie's wrists with the duct tape and used the rope he held on Tina's.

"Sit with your back to the car," he demanded of Tina, and then set about tying her ankles together when she'd complied.

Once both women were secured, Levi pulled a knife from his sock and cut Leslie's clothes from her body.

Huge tears poured from Leslie's eyes, paling only in comparison to the pleading spilling from her lips.

Her words fell on deaf ears.

Levi moved around her, his eyes as deadpan as his voice. He slowly peeled off his shirt in a deliberate manner meant to incite fear. It worked.

Leslie frantically shook her head, backing up until she lost her footing on the uneven earth and toppled over onto her back.

She cried out in agony. With her hands restrained behind her, it was obvious her shoulders took the brunt of the fall.

Levi laid the gun on the ground and unzipped his jeans, stalking forward with calculated steps.

Tina had to do something—anything to prevent him from doing what she knew he would do. "It must make you feel awfully powerful to hurt someone smaller than you!"

He stilled, his head cranking in her direction. His eyes glittered from beneath hooded lids, but he didn't speak.

Tina spit in his direction. "You're a real big man, aren't you, Levi? Or is it Gary? Did you steal the name Levi also? I bet you have a typical name. Probably something like Dahmer. Or Bundy. Some lame—"

He lunged at her, cutting off the rest of her words.

Holding her chin in a painful grip, he growled, "Do not ever lump me up in the same category as Dahmer. I'm no cannibal."

He said that as if raping and stabbing someone to death were any better. But Tina was far too terrified to point that out. Between the painful hold he had on her face and the insane look swirling in his eyes, she knew he would kill her instantly.

Leslie somehow managed to get to her feet. She began running in the direction of the main road, naked, with no shoes and her arms restrained behind her back.

Levi surged upward and took off after her. He caught up with her in a few short strides.

Tina dropped her head back against the car, watching through her tears as Levi dragged the redhead back to the place she'd originally fallen.

He threw her to the ground, flipped her over, and fell on top of her.

"Please don't!" Leslie cried, her voice high-pitched with panic. Her cries only fueled him on.

He thrust forward violently, forcing a hoarse scream from his victim.

Tina squeezed her eyes shut, unable to bear the scene taking place in front of her.

The horrific sounds coming from Leslie were matched only by the sickening grunts Levi made as he cruelly assaulted her.

Tina's body shook against that car, and her lungs felt as if they had collapsed inside her chest. The tears had long since stopped falling, and nothing remained but the unholy sounds of Leslie's moans.

A gurgling noise soon followed, forcing Tina's hot, swollen eyes to fly open.

She stared in horror at the sight of Leslie, now lying on her back, dirt covering the front of her body, and bright red blood gushing from her neck.

"Oh God, noooooooo," Tina groaned deep in her throat. "No…"

Chapter Seventeen

"We got a hit on Miss Duggar's SUV," the sheriff announced, poking his head around the corner of the room Mike currently paced in.

Mike rushed to the door, his heart in his throat. "Any sign of Tina?"

The sheriff shook his head. "Only the vehicle. It was found at a store a few miles west of Marianna. The Jackson County Sheriff's Office is processing the vehicle now."

"The driver's side door of the SUV had been left open," Wilcox continued. "When the store clerk went out to investigate, he found a large amount of blood on one of the back seats."

Mike's stomach lurched. Did that blood belong to Tina? He prayed to God it didn't.

He had to clear his throat in order to speak around the lump forming there. "How long ago did the clerk notice the SUV?"

"He told one of the deputies that the vehicle wasn't there when he went to stock the bathroom. He noticed it approximately ten minutes later when he stepped out to have a cigarette."

A tiny spark of hope flared to life inside Mike. "How long ago was that?"

"About twenty minutes ago."

"Security footage?"

"Yes."

Mike ran a hand through his hair, exhaling in relief. Hopefully, the video footage would show them what had happened at that store.

"Let's see what the security cameras show," the sheriff murmured, touching Mike on the arm. "They're forwarding us a copy now."

Mike had to force himself to remain calm when he felt anything but. He stalked behind the sheriff to a corner office.

Wilcox rounded a table and sat in a chair facing a computer screen. His fingers pecked around on the keyboard until the video file appeared before them.

Opening the file, Wilcox clicked on play.

A video came to life, revealing Tina's black SUV wheeling into the parking lot of a gas station.

Mike's heart ached watching it. He wanted to reach through that screen and snatch her out, to remove her from harm's way.

"There," Wilcox practically barked, freezing the footage.

A man's blurred and grainy face appeared on the screen. He sat in the passenger seat of Tina's SUV, staring straight ahead.

Tina's unclear image could also be seen. Though Mike couldn't see clearly, he would know her features anywhere.

The vehicle disappeared around the side of the building.

Mike leaned in over the sheriff's shoulder, watching as a red-haired woman wearing shorts and a tank top exited the store. She also disappeared around the corner.

Minutes ticked by when a green, four-door car left the parking lot with three heads inside.

Wilcox froze the image, clicking several times in an effort to enlarge it.

Mike grabbed a pen and paper, quickly jotting down the tag number of that car. "I can't thank you enough, Sheriff." He headed for the door.

"Parker?" the sheriff called before Mike made it out.

Stopping to look back over his shoulder, Mike met the sheriff's gaze. "Sir?"

"I hope you find her."

Mike didn't trust his voice. He sent Wilcox a nod and hurried from the station.

Once in his car, Mike backed from the parking lot, already phoning the Jackson County Sheriff's Office.

"This is Investigator Mike Parker with the Bay County Sheriff's Office," he barked the second the dispatcher answered the phone. "I'm en route to you from Lake City. The SUV you're processing belongs to my fiancé."

He'd just referred to Tina as his fiancé. In a sense, she was. Or she would be when he proposed. And he would propose. Just as soon as he had her safely in his arms again.

Mike went on to explain the situation to the dispatcher, who promptly put him in touch with Austin Cannon, the investigator overseeing the situation with the blood-filled SUV.

Cannon and Mike spoke for close to twenty minutes, with the other man filling Mike in on what had been discovered inside the SUV. They also went over the video footage of the green four-door leaving the scene.

"We've already sent out a BOLO to FHP and surrounding counties for that green car," Cannon assured him.

Mike let that sink in. "My guess is they're heading west on Interstate 10."

Cannon readily agreed. "We've notified Bay and Walton County as well."

"That's where I'm headed now," Mike informed him. "Call me the second you hear something."

"Will do." Cannon ended the call.

Mike accelerated toward the interstate. *Where are you, Tina...*

Chapter Eighteen

Tina's mind had long ago gone numb. She stared straight ahead as Levi straightened his clothes.

He zipped up his pants, picked up the gun, and then tucked the knife inside his sock. The gun went into the waistband of his jeans.

"Don't look so desolate," he teased, moving to kneel down next to her. "It's really unbecoming of one with your spirit."

Spirit? Tina thought in a clouded haze. She doubted she had any spirit left in her. Something inside her had died with Roslynn. And the rest of her humanity had been severed by the brutal rape and slaughter of the innocent woman lying not far from her feet. "Go to Hell."

Levi laughed, throwing his leg over hers to straddle her.

Tina turned her face away, regretting that she had provoked him.

"I'm already in Hell, Tina. Can't you see that?"

"Why don't you just kill me and get it over with?" She wasn't sure where the words spilling from her mouth were coming from, but she seemed powerless to stop them. "You're going to do it eventually. Just do it already. I'd rather die than spend one more minute in your disgusting company."

He cupped her head in his hands, forcing her to face him. "You will die when *I'm* ready for you to die. Not when *you* say. *I* say, Tina. I say." He slanted his mouth across hers.

Tina bit him. She sank her teeth into his bottom lip as hard as she could.

Levi roared. He slammed his fist against her temple, sending excruciating pain shooting through her skull.

Her head flew to the side, forcing her to release her hold on his mouth.

His hand went to his injured mouth. Blood oozed between the cracks of his fingers. "You wanna play dirty? Let's play."

"Oh God," Tina whispered in fear. He planned to hurt her.

She forced back the plea that rose in her throat. She wouldn't beg him. No matter what he did to her.

Still straddling her, he reached down and tugged the knife from his sock, flipping it open with one hand.

Tina's gaze instinctively went to that blade now moving closer to her face. Fear unlike anything she'd ever known took control of her. It dominated her nervous system, sending her body into full-on panic mode.

She trembled violently. But God help her, she didn't beg.

He brought the tip of that blade to rest beneath her left eye. "You have incredible eyes, Tina."

Applying pressure, he leaned in closer. "Just like Renee's."

Tina felt the instant that blade penetrated her skin. She gritted her teeth together to keep from crying out.

A warm droplet of blood trailed down her cheek. Still, she didn't beg.

Her lack of reaction angered him. He dragged the knife along her cheek, cutting a track down to her chin. The pain became overwhelming, as if a hot poker had burned its way along her flesh.

Though her entire body shook with excruciating pain, Tina's mind scrambled to find a way of escape.

She blurted the first thing that came to mind. "W-who is Renee?"

That gave him pause. "What do you know about Renee?"

Tina could barely speak through her closed throat. "Her…" She swallowed and tried again. "Her name is tattooed on your fingers." She didn't point out that he'd mentioned she and Renee had similar eyes.

Levi's gaze grew even crazier, if that were possible. "She's dead."

That wasn't what Tina wanted to hear. He'd obviously killed this Renee. Just as he would kill Tina. But if she could keep him talking… "What happened to her?"

Levi twitched, the manic expression on his face more terrifying than the knife he held.

His eyes grew distant, the hand holding the blade falling away from Tina's face. "It was an accident."

Tina's heart pounded erratically. If she pushed him too far, he would probably stab her to death. Yet what choice did she have? She was dead either way. At least if she kept him talking, it bought her a little more time. Time for what, she didn't know. She doubted anyone would discover them in the remote location they were currently in. But she had to try.

"Did you kill her?"

Rage flashed in his blue eyes. "You think I would harm my own child?"

Tina licked her lips. "Renee was pregnant when she died?"

Levi sat back on Tina's bound legs, his weight cutting off her circulation. "She didn't want the baby. She'd made an appointment to abort it. When I refused her, she ran off to her mother's in Tennessee."

His gaze grew even more distant. "She never made it. Her car went off a cliff along the mountain. Her body was never recovered."

"She was your wife?" Tina asked in a trembling whisper.

Levi merely nodded. And then, his expression blanked. "You're trying to get inside my head."

"No," Tina rushed out, realizing she'd gone too far.

The knife was suddenly at her throat. "Your time is up, Tina."

Sirens could suddenly be heard in the distance.

Levi stilled, swiveling his head in the direction of the sound.

He bounded to his feet and cut the ropes free from Tina's ankles.

Yanking her up, he spun her around, her stomach slamming against the side of the car. Her hands were cut loose as well.

"Get in," he demanded, impatience lining his voice.

Tina didn't argue. She stumbled around and got in the driver's side.

Levi slid into the passenger seat. "Let's go."

Backing up to avoid running over Leslie's bloodied form, Tina put the car in drive and eased down the dirt road.

"Once we make it to the highway," Levi announced, glancing around in all directions, "I want you to take a left. We need to change vehicles."

Tina's heart sank. She knew the police were likely looking for them. And they would know what type of car they were in by now. Changing transportation would prolong the search.

The gun was suddenly in Levi's hand. "Do what I said."

Tina took a left at the highway.

"Drive the speed limit."

"I am," she whispered, petrified of that gun aimed in her direction. If his finger accidently slipped...

"Turn into that drive up ahead on the right."

Tina did as he instructed, noticing a two-story house at the end of the drive, with two vehicles parked out front.

"Stop the car," Levi ordered, returning the gun to the waistband of his jeans. "And get out. One wrong move, and I'll kill everyone in that house. Got it?"

Tina nodded, put the car in park, and climbed out.

Levi followed tight on her heels.

"Go knock on the door."

Nausea rolled. "Please don't hurt these people."

He shoved her forward. "Shut up and do as I say!"

Moving up the walkway, Tina stopped on the porch. She lifted a hand to knock but couldn't bring herself to do it. "Don't do this."

Levi growled an obscenity from behind her, leaned over her shoulder, and rapped his knuckles on the door.

The knob turned, and a middle-aged man appeared in the now open doorway. "Yes? Can I help you?"

Levi shot him.

The deafening explosion forced a bloodcurdling scream from Tina.

She stared in horror at the bullet hole in the man's forehead. He dropped heavily at her feet.

Another scream came from the interior of the house, followed by a pale-faced woman staggering around the corner.

"Anthony?" the woman cried, her gaze going to her husband's lifeless body.

Levi shot again, the bullet hitting its mark.

Tina's knees buckled beneath her. She rocked back and forth, her brain unable to process the scene before her. Levi had killed the older couple.

Suddenly grabbing her by the arm, Levi forced her back to her feet. He led her through the foyer, leaving her no choice but to step over the two dead bodies. "Find the car keys."

Find the what? Tina thought, her brain too scrambled to understand what he wanted from her.

He didn't answer, only gave her a shove, sending her slipping through the blood beneath her shoes.

"Here they are." Levi snatched a set of keys from a hook on the wall and guided Tina back to the door.

Tina jumped when a beep sounded next to her.

"This one." Levi pushed her toward a small, white SUV. He handed her the keys.

Opening the car door, Tina slid behind the wheel and started the engine while Levi took up the passenger seat.

She put on her seatbelt and backed from the drive, her mind too numb to do anything else.

Chapter Nineteen

Mike arrived back in Bay County, his cell phone still in hand.

He'd been on the phone with every surrounding county for a hundred miles. He had also kept in contact with the Florida Highway Patrol. They were combing the interstate, searching for the green four-door, license plate number WYG27A.

Tina was still alive. Mike had seen her silhouette in the green car leaving that store.

He had never been more grateful for the security camera at that gas station. Without it, they would have had no clue what vehicle Tina had been in.

"Parker?" Sheriff Mulligan called out, heading in Mike's direction.

He clapped a hand on Mike's shoulder. "We'll find her. You can bet on it."

Mike had known Mulligan for twenty years. The man had been the sheriff of Bay County, Florida for as long as Mike could remember.

"How are you holding up?" Mulligan asked, giving Mike's shoulder a gentle squeeze.

Mike sucked in some much-needed air. "Not good, sir. This is the hardest thing I've ever been through. Tina is in the clutches of a maniac. And I can't do anything about it."

"You're doing something. We have every available man in every county from Lake City to Alabama, Mississippi, and Georgia looking for her. We'll find her."

Mike wanted to believe that. He *needed* to believe it. Hope was all he had at the moment.

Investigator Desiree Lenore appeared at Mike's elbow, a cup of steaming coffee in hand. "Here, drink this. Have you eaten anything today?"

Eaten? Food was the last thing on Mike's mind. But he also knew he needed to eat to keep up his strength.

He shook his head. "Not yet."

"Come on," Desiree prompted, nodding toward the breakroom. "I have some stuff in the fridge."

Mike followed the investigator into the breakroom. He took a seat at the small table in the center of the room and dropped his head into his hands.

The beeping sounds of a microwave echoed throughout the room.

"It's just some leftover casserole I made last night," Desiree murmured, removing the food from the microwave and setting it in front of Mike.

He lifted his head. "It looks good. Thank you, Des."

"You're welcome. Now eat. Please. You won't do Tina any good if you end up sick."

Nodding his thanks, Mike picked up the fork Desiree had placed beside the plate and took a bite without tasting it.

Desiree pulled out a chair across the table from him and sat. "Let's think about this rationally. The man Tina is with has kept her alive for a reason. She's smart, Mike. And strong. One of the strongest women I know."

Mike didn't have to be told how strong Tina was. Nor how smart. He'd been seeing her for three years. He planned on spending the rest of his life with her. Camping, fishing, laughing together. "I know."

Desiree continued to talk, her voice a calming presence in Mike's otherwise chaotic mind.

He looked across the table at her, his eyes conveying the appreciation his mouth couldn't seem to speak.

She seemed to get the message, if her expression were any indication.

Sheriff Mulligan suddenly appeared in the doorway. "Bobbi Deloach has been found alive."

Grateful, Mike asked, "Is she all right?"

"I believe so. She was found in Marianna. She's at a hospital there. Her husband has been notified and is on his way there now."

"Did she say anything about Tina? If she's hurt or…?"

The sheriff's gaze softened. "That's all I know at the moment. But there's something else. A shooting was reported in Jackson County. The deputies on scene discovered the green four-door."

Mike surged to his feet.

"Neither of the bodies are hers," the sheriff rushed out, obviously realizing Mike's terror.

Relief poured through Mike, nearly buckling his legs.

The sheriff continued. "The homeowners were killed, one of their vehicles stolen. A small, white SUV." He rattled off the make, model, and license plate number. "FHP and the surrounding counties have been notified. Lake County got a hit on the fingerprints pulled from Tina's vehicle. The man who took her is Levi Ransom."

Mike narrowed his eyes. "Priors?"

"A list as long as my arm. We're looking for possible relatives, friends, etcetera, in the area that might shed some light on this lunatic."

Mike headed for the door. "Let's see that rap sheet."

Chapter Twenty

Tina couldn't stop her shaking. Levi had murdered two more people. Two innocent people who happened to be unfortunate enough to cross his path.

They meant nothing to him besides a means of inflicting pain. He enjoyed hurting others. Tina had seen it in his eyes every time he'd taken a life.

What could have possibly happened to him that would cause him to take joy in hurting others? "Were you abused as a child?"

She regretted the words the second they left her mouth.

His head snapped around and the gun with it. "Why would you say that?"

Tina held the steering wheel in a white-knuckled grip, her gaze touching on a sign for Panama City. Mike was out there, near, and yet so far. "I'm just trying to understand you. Killing people isn't normal. Something had to happen to—"

"Shut up!" he snapped, spittle flying from his mouth. "You don't know anything about me!"

Tina gripped the wheel tighter in an effort to keep her arms from visibly shaking. "I want to."

"Don't you dare patronize me!" He pulled the hammer back on the gun.

He's going to kill me. Tina glanced hysterically in his direction. The look on his face said it all. The man staring back at her had a deadness in his eyes. A deadness that promised retribution.

"Get off the interstate."

Tears surfaced. She couldn't leave the safety of the interstate.

"I said, get off," he bit out in a deadly soft voice.

She bypassed the exit.

His lips peeled back over his teeth. He abruptly released his seatbelt and lunged at her, his face mere inches from her own. "If you don't stop this car, I will cut you into pieces while you drive. Starting with your eyes."

Tina didn't think beyond the fact that he'd removed his seatbelt. If she were going to die in that car, then she would take him with her.

She jerked the wheel, hard right, sending the small SUV off the road toward a power pole.

The last thing Tina saw before agony and darkness overtook her was the sight of Levi flying through the windshield.

He'd been ejected.

* * * *

Tina moaned deep in her throat. Where was she? Her head hurt something fierce, and a stabbing pain in her thigh brought her fully awake.

Her eyelids slowly opened to reveal millions of stars forming in the sky. How had it become dark?

A man's voice spoke from somewhere nearby. "Ma'am? Stay with me, ma'am. Help is on the way."

Ma'am? Who would be referring to her as ma'am?

And then memory came flooding back with a vengeance.

Panicked, Tina attempted to sit up, but strong hands held her down. "Don't try to move. Your leg is bleeding pretty bad. I tied it off as best I could, but I'm not sure how long it'll hold. My name is Dave."

"Where is he?" Tina whispered, her gaze frantically scanning the area.

The one known as Dave leaned in above her. "Where is whom? Was there someone with you? I searched the surrounding area but didn't find anyone else."

"There was a man with me," was all she could manage before the sound of sirens echoed in the distance.

"Are you sure?" Dave pressed, turning his head from left to right. "Maybe they went for help. There's no one here but you and me."

Levi was gone. Which meant, he still lived.

Tina attempted to sit up again. "We have to get out of here before he comes back."

When Dave tried to hold her down once more, she screamed in his face, "Let me go! The man that was with me has a gun, and he's killed four people that I know of! Now move!"

Dave paled, his mouth dropping open in shock. "You're the one I heard about on the news. You're Tina Duggar."

So, they did know of her abduction, Tina thought, realizing that Mike also knew and had to be frantic by now.

A patrol car slid to a stop along the side of the road, followed by another and then an ambulance.

Tina laid her head back in the grass, relieved beyond words to see the deputies running in her direction.

She was finally safe…

Chapter Twenty-One

Mike drove at a high rate of speed to the Bay County Memorial Hospital in Panama City Beach.

Tina had survived.

He had no idea how badly she might be injured; he only knew that she lived. And if he himself lived to be a hundred, he would never let her out of his sight again.

Mike had already made the decision to retire from law enforcement, make Tina his bride, and give her the life that she deserved.

His mind turned to the man who'd abducted her. Levi Ransom. He hadn't been with Tina when she'd been found.

Had the maniac simply let her go, or had she escaped somehow? Mike didn't know, but he intended to find out. If he had to hunt the monster for the rest of his life, Mike would find Levi Ransom…and he would kill him.

The hospital came into view approximately twenty minutes later.

Mike pulled into an empty spot close to the front, jumped out, and jogged through the automatic doors.

"May I help you?" an elderly woman asked from behind a glass window.

Mike flashed his badge. "Can you tell me where I can find Tina Duggar?"

The woman took longer than what Mike thought necessary to look at his badge before typing in something on the computer in front of her. "Miss Duggar is in surgery on the third floor."

"Thank you." Mike hurried off to the elevators.

Tina was in surgery. How badly had she been hurt? Anxiety mixed with fear inside him. He couldn't lose her now. He *wouldn't*.

Taking the elevator to the third floor, Mike stepped into the hall and approached the nurses' desk.

Once again, he flashed his badge. "Tina Duggar. Can you tell me how she's doing?"

A young, blonde nurse looked up from some papers she'd been sifting through. "She's still in surgery. There's a waiting area down the hall there, if you'd like to wait."

"Is she going to be okay?" Mike pressed, ignoring the suggestion he go wait down the hall.

The nurse's gaze softened. "The doctor will do everything he can to make sure she's all right. Why don't you go have a seat and try to relax? I'll come get you the moment she's out of surgery."

Relax? She honestly thought he could relax?

Mike thanked the nurse and strode off to wait in the designated room.

He unclipped his cell phone and dialed Sheriff Mulligan's number.

"Mulligan."

"Hey, Sheriff, it's Mike. Any news on Levi Ransom?"

The sheriff answered without hesitation. "Nothing yet, but there's a massive manhunt going on, and the FBI has been called in. With the man discovered in the trunk of his car at that rest stop, and the four others Ransom allegedly killed, that makes him a serial killer. How's Tina?"

"She's in surgery. I don't know anything more."

"She'll be okay, Mike. Just hang in there. I'm getting ready to head home for the night. Desiree is out at the interstate, processing the scene of the accident. Hopefully, she finds something out there that will help us locate this monster. She said it appeared someone had been ejected from the vehicle. Since Tina had been wearing her seatbelt, that leaves Ransom."

Mike wanted to jump in his car, drive out there, and comb through those woods. But he couldn't. He refused to leave Tina.

* * * *

"Sir?" the blonde nurse called out, appearing in the doorway to the waiting room. "Miss Duggar is out of surgery now."

"Is she okay?"

"She's going to be just fine," the nurse assured him with a smile.

Mike nearly slid to the floor in relief. "May I see her?"

"Sure. Follow me."

Mike hurried from the room to trail along next to the tiny nurse. Tina had survived.

After taking at least three different hallways, the nurse hit a large, silver button on the wall, and a set of double doors swung inward.

The smell of antiseptic wafted out, along with a blast of icy-cold air. They had arrived in the recovery area.

Another nurse approached, her dark hair pulled up on top of her head in a severe bun. A gold rectangle nametag rested over her right breast pocket, with an engraving that read, BRENDA RN.

The two women spoke for a moment, and then the blonde left the room.

Brenda softly smiled. "Are you a family member of Miss Duggar's?"

"I'm her fiancé." Mike felt zero remorse for the small lie. Tina would be his wife in the very near future. At least, he prayed she would.

The nurse went on to explain the condition Tina was brought in with. "A piece of metal had punctured her thigh, nicking her femoral artery. Which the doctor was able to repair. She also had some deep lacerations that required stitches."

Mike listened intently as the nurse walked him through Tina's condition before she pulled back the curtain Tina lay behind, allowing him to see her.

"I'll give you some privacy," Brenda whispered, turning and disappearing from view.

Mike locked his teeth together to keep from cursing aloud. His precious Tina had almost been killed.

Bruises and swelling were obvious on her face, and a long white bandage covered the length of her jaw.

He wanted to lift her from that bed and take her home. To hold and protect her, to never allow her to be hurt again.

Her leg was propped up on some pillows, a large amount of gauze wrapped around her thigh. Her femoral artery had been cut. She would have bled out if someone hadn't stopped to help her in time.

Mike leaned in close and tenderly pressed his lips to her forehead. He gently took hold of her hand, noticing one of her fingernails had been broken to the quick.

His mind rebelled against thoughts of what she'd endured at the hands of that maniac. He couldn't allow himself to go there for fear of breaking down in front of her.

No matter what she'd endured, he would help her through it. She was his to take care of, his to love, and his to protect. And he would protect her at any cost for the rest of his natural life.

A soft moan escaped Tina. Her fingers tightened around his, and her head began to roll from side to side.

"Nurse?" Mike called out, his heart in his throat.

Brenda came rushing over, a syringe in hand. She injected the contents into Tina's IV, then lifted one of her eyelids, then the other.

Mike watched helplessly as Brenda moved around the bed, checking Tina's vitals and extremities.

In less than a minute, Tina calmed.

"Is she okay?" Mike asked in a low tone, anxiety evident in his voice.

Brenda nodded. "The mind doesn't always shut down completely. Especially when there's trauma involved. I gave her something to help her relax. She should sleep comfortably for a bit. I'll get you a chair if you'd like to stay with her."

"Yes, please." Mike had no intention of leaving her side. Ever again.

Chapter Twenty-Two

Pain. A deep, throbbing pain dominated Tina's thigh. Her face hurt almost as much, only it stung as if alcohol had been poured over a cut.

Her eyelids felt heavy, and her mouth as dry as cotton.

A beeping noise came from her right to blend with other strange sounds in the distance.

She groaned against the pain in her body and forced her heavy lids apart.

Bright light shone from above her, forcing her to squint against it. Where was she?

And then memory returned. Levi… Roslynn's nude, bloody body lying on that dirt road. Bobbi being stripped and left somewhere in the woods. Leslie, the redhead unfortunate enough to be at the store that Levi forced Tina to stop behind. She'd been brutally raped in the same fashion as Roslynn. Her throat slit. The older couple that had been shot inside their home…

A strangled sound left Tina's throat.

"Tina?" Mike's face appeared above her, the most precious and handsome face she'd ever seen.

"Mike," she choked out, needing his arms around her. If he could just hold her close, she would wake from her nightmare.

He pressed his lips against hers, his own eyes suspiciously moist. "Thank God you're okay. I've never been so worried in all my life. I thought I'd lost you…"

A tear slipped from the corner of Tina's eye. "Roslynn's dead…"

Mike reached up and tucked some stray hairs behind her ear. "I know. I'm so sorry, baby."

"Have they caught him yet?" Tina managed to ask around the lump in her throat.

Mike shook his head. "Not yet, but they will. The FBI has been called in. There's a nationwide manhunt happening right now. They will catch him. I promise you that."

Another tear fell. "The things he did to Roslynn…"

"Shhhh," Mike gently shushed her. "You don't have to talk about that right now."

Tina continued, unable to do anything else. "He raped her, Mike. For hours, he brutally raped her. He stabbed her so many times. I could hear it, Mike. I'll never forget the sounds she made."

Gazing up into Mike's eyes, Tina whispered brokenly, "I was terrified that I would be next. I remember begging God not to let me be next while that monster hurt Roslynn."

Unable to cope with the memories a second longer, Tina openly cried.

Mike laid his face against her uninjured cheek. "Shhhhh. I'm so sorry. Please don't cry."

"I was so relieved that he didn't hurt me," Tina whispered through her tears. "How could I feel relief after what happened to Roslynn?"

Pulling back, Mike wiped at Tina's tears with his thumbs. "Because you're human. You were afraid. Anyone would have felt the same in your position."

Tina shook her head, the movement causing pain in her face. "I can't take it back. I can never take it back…"

"Baby, listen to me," Mike implored her, his eyes conveying his helpless torment. "None of this is your fault. You have to—"

"I let him in," she interrupted, her voice growing in volume. "I knew better. I should have never given him a ride."

Her mind drifted back to the rest area where she had first met Levi. She thought about how normal he'd seemed, how harmless.

And then another memory surfaced. "Gary. Gary Rowland. The car Levi was driving when we met him. It belonged to a man named Gary Rowland."

Mike's expression turned serious. "We know about Rowland."

"And...and this woman named Leslie. The older couple—he shot this older couple in their home."

"I know, baby. But I do have some good news."

Tina blinked rapidly in an attempt to see through her tears. "Tell me."

"Bobbi was found alive."

"Oh my God," Tina breathed, her relief so great she became dizzy with it. "He left her in the woods with her hands tied. Where is she?"

"She's at the hospital in Marianna. Her husband should be there with her now."

Tina let that sink in. "He didn't hurt her. He was going to, but he let her go when she begged for the life of her unborn baby."

Mike's eyebrows lifted. "Bobbi's pregnant?"

"Yes. And I had no idea. She never said anything."

A dark-haired nurse approached the bed, a gentle smile on her face. "Miss Duggar? My name is Brenda. How are you feeling?"

"Like I've been hit by a truck."

Brenda went about checking Tina's bandage. "We have a room ready for you on the second floor."

Tina wanted to go home. "How long will I have to stay in the hospital?"

"That depends. You had a piece of metal buried in your thigh when you arrived. It nicked your femoral artery. The doctor was able to repair it, but I'm sure he's going to want you to stay for a couple of days to be sure that no problems arise."

The nurse patted Tina on the arm. "We want you to get better."

Tina knew her body would heal in time. It was her mind she had doubts about.

Chapter Twenty-Three

One week later

Mike brought Tina's medications to the recliner she sat in. He handed her the pills, along with a glass of water. "You look better today."

Tina popped the pills into her mouth, washed them down with the water, and then set the glass on the end table next to her.

Her fingers lifted to feel along the cut on her cheek. "This will always be a reminder."

Mike shook his head. "The doctor said as long as you use the scar repair cream, it shouldn't leave a scar."

He glanced at the pink line running the length of her cheek. "I saw the vehicle you were driving. You're very fortunate to be alive."

Tina looked away. "I didn't get this from the accident."

Mike's stomach flipped. "Do you feel like talking about it?"

She remained quiet so long he wondered if she'd shut him out. And then, "He cut me. Held a knife to my face and…cut me."

Mike lowered to his haunches next to her chair. He didn't speak, only touched her on the arm as a show of support.

Tina continued. "I've never known terror like I felt in his presence. He had an evil inside him that was suffocating. His eyes…"

Still, Mike didn't speak. She needed to talk; he could sense it as surely as he could feel her pain.

"He spoke in a deadpan voice, as if he had no humanity inside him… As if he were already dead and had nothing left to lose."

She took a shuddering breath. "The only time he showed even an ounce of humanity was when he let Bobbi go free."

Mike noticed a small indention appear between Tina's eyes.

She softly murmured, "He told me that his pregnant wife had left him, that she'd had an accident on her way to her mother's. Her car went off the side of the mountain. I wonder if that's what made his mind snap."

Tina slowly turned her head in Mike's direction. "Her name was Renee. He said I reminded him of her."

Mike's fingers drew lazy circles on her arm. "Who knows what his reasons were for doing the terrible things he did. He's demented, a psychopath."

"But a psychopath doesn't feel empathy for others. Yet, he let Bobbi go after hearing about her pregnancy."

"You're overthinking it, baby. No one fully understands the mind of a psychopath. If he had an ounce of empathy, he wouldn't have hurt the others. Maybe Bobbi triggered something inside him. You said his wife was pregnant when she died. It most likely had something to do with that. We will never know the answer to that. All we can do is try to move beyond what happened."

"I know," Tina whispered, laying her head back against the recliner. "Because if I can't, then he's still holding me hostage."

Mike straightened and kissed her on the forehead. "Can I get you anything? Are you hungry?"

Tina shook her head. "I'm just going to rest my eyes. You don't have to hover. I'll be fine."

The corner of his mouth lifted. "You think I'm hovering?"

"A little," she teased, smiling in return.

"Okay, I'll be in my office," he replied, giving her arm a gentle squeeze. "Maybe I can get some work done."

Tina covered his hand with hers. "After I nap for a bit, I'd like to go see the house your father left you. If you feel up to it."

"I feel up to doing anything you want to do. Rest, and I'll take you over there this afternoon."

She closed her eyes. "Sounds good."

Mike trailed to his office in the back of the house and took a seat behind his desk. He plucked up his cell phone and dialed Desiree.

"Hey," she answered on the first ring. She obviously recognized his number or had him stored in her contacts. "How's Tina?"

"She's getting better. Moving a little slow, but she's been putting weight on the leg without too much of a limp."

Desiree made a relieved sound in the back of her throat. "That's good to hear. What about emotionally? She's been through one heck of a trauma."

"She's struggling," Mike softly admitted. "It kills me to see the uncertainty and pain in her eyes."

Desiree grew quiet for a moment. "It's going to take time to heal. She may need to talk to someone."

"You mean like a psychiatrist?"

"Yes."

Mike thought about Tina's reaction to him suggesting a mental health specialist. "I'm not sure how she'll feel about that, but you're right. She probably does need to see one. I'll mention it to her when the moment's right. Any word from the FBI?"

"You mean on the hitcher?"

So, the psychopath had been dubbed *the hitcher*. "Yes."

"Nothing yet. If I had to guess, he's probably ten states over by now."

That wasn't what Mike wanted to hear. "He'll turn up. They always do."

A beeping sound came through the line, telling Mike that he had a call waiting. "I got another call. Keep me posted."

"Will do."

Mike pressed the button that would switch him over to the incoming call. "Parker."

"Hi, Mike, it's Karen. Sorry to bother you at home, but I wanted to check on Tina, and I was afraid to call her cell in case she was sleeping."

Mike repeated everything he'd told Desiree. "I'll be sure to let her know you called."

"Thank you," Karen murmured. "Also, I wasn't sure if you heard, but the judge did sign that warrant to search Sonny Jenkins' place. We found the injured dogs. The narcissistic idiot wasn't smart enough to move them. We found the breaking sticks, blood, and several more pieces of damning evidence in a shed out back.

He's been arrested, and the dogs have been seized."

"That's good to hear. Although it won't stop him from obtaining more dogs in the future. At least you were able to rescue the ones in his possession."

Karen sighed through the phone. "I know. Well, give Tina my love and let her know we all miss her up here."

"I will, Karen. And she misses you too." Mike ended the call.

Chapter Twenty-Four

Tina eased the footrest down on the recliner and slowly pushed to a standing position.

The initial weight put on her leg sent a dull pain snaking through her thigh. But it was bearable. And the more she walked on it, the easier it got.

She moved across the room in search of Mike. The floor beneath her bare feet felt cool, soothing, somehow.

The sound of snoring reached her ears the closer she got to Mike's office.

She found him sitting at his desk, his head resting on top of his folded arms. He'd fallen asleep.

Trailing into the office, she inched up behind him, intending on sending him to bed.

His laptop had been left open.

She slid her finger across the mouse pad to see what he'd been working on. The screen came to life.

An image of a mangled car that had been crushed to the point of resembling a beer can appeared before her.

Her gaze lifted to the headline to find the story about Renee Ransom's car going over a cliff. And just as Levi had told her, Renee's body had never been found.

A picture of Renee rested at the top of the article. She appeared to be in her late twenties, early thirties. Black hair. Though Tina couldn't see her eye color, she knew they were hazel. She also saw the resemblance to herself.

A strange sensation slid through Tina. Could Renee have faked her death to get away from a monster? If she'd been pregnant, she might. Or had Levi killed her and dumped her car off that cliff?

Mike suddenly stirred a second before sitting up. He stared straight ahead for a moment and then looked over his shoulder. "Hey, you. How long have you been here?"

Tina met his gaze. "Not long. Why were you looking into the death of Renee Ransom?" But she knew. He'd wondered the same thing as her.

Mike blew out a breath. "I was just thinking about what you told me, about her body never being found. Something felt off about it."

Tina rested her hand on his shoulder. "I know. If it had been anyone else, I wouldn't question it. But I find it odd that her car went over a cliff as she was trying to leave that maniac."

Moving around to the side, she waited for Mike to push his chair back and open his arms.

Tina lowered herself to his lap. "What if he killed her and made it look like an accident?"

"My thoughts exactly," Mike murmured, nuzzling her shoulder. "Or she did it in an attempt to escape him."

"I'd thought of that too."

Tina grew quiet for a moment. "How do you feel about taking a road trip?"

Mike abandoned his nuzzling to gape at her. "In your condition?"

"I'm fine. The leg is actually tolerable. Besides, we can take the motorhome and pull the car behind it. I can sleep while you drive."

"You're serious?" He'd yet to stop gaping.

Tina nodded. "As I've ever been. I say we go pay a visit to Renee's mother. It won't hurt to ask her a few questions. It might give us some insight into this weirdo. Maybe help locate him. You've taken some time off. What do we have to lose?"

Mike ran a hand down his face. "Are you sure you can handle something like that? The man tried to kill you."

A memory of Levi holding that knife to her eye flashed through her mind, followed by Roslynn's torture and death.

Tina shuddered. "If I sit here and do nothing, I'll only relive it over and over. I need the distraction. And hopefully, we'll find out something that will help."

Mike pulled her close. "I don't want you hurt anymore. And I think it's too soon for you to be traveling."

"I'm a big girl, Mike. If I didn't think I could do it, I wouldn't."

"Okay. I'll get the motorhome ready. We'll leave first thing in the morning."

Tina slid off his lap. "I'm going to find something to eat."

"Nonsense," Mike gently scolded, gaining his feet. "You rest. I'll have something delivered. Any requests?"

Tina moved toward the door. "Anything with cheese."

"Pizza it is."

"I'm going to shower while you order the food." Tina made her way down the hall to Mike's big bathroom.

She switched on the water, peeled out of her clothes, and stepped under the hot, steaming spray.

In the privacy of the bathroom, the brave face she'd attempted to hide behind in front of Mike slipped completely.

Truth was, she saw Levi Ransom every time she closed her eyes. She even conjured him up in her waking moments.

She needed him to be found, to be punished. And if going to Tennessee to find out the truth about Renee's death would help accomplish that, then that's exactly what she had to do.

Reliving the terror of being in Levi's clutches was slowly chipping away at Tina's sanity. She couldn't get Roslynn off her mind. Her muffled screams haunted Tina day and night.

Nausea rolled, forcing her to breathe deeply or risk vomiting.

She'd attended Roslynn's funeral in a wheelchair. Saying her final goodbyes had been one of the hardest things she'd ever had to do.

Bobbi hadn't been present, but Tina hadn't expected her to be. Her doctor had ordered bed rest for a few weeks to be sure she didn't miscarry.

According to Joey, Bobbi had been spotting when she'd arrived at the hospital. Which wasn't surprising after everything she'd been through.

Tina prayed nightly for Bobbi to carry her baby to term. Losing it would destroy her.

"The food will be here in about twenty minutes," Mike announced, opening the bathroom door.

He poked his head around the shower curtain. "Are you okay?"

Tina wiped the water from her face. "I was just thinking about Roslynn and Bobbi. It's still hard to believe that Roz is gone. I'll never get the chance to see her again."

Mike stepped over the side of the tub, clothes and all. He wrapped her in his arms, pulling her face against his shoulder.

He didn't speak. He didn't need to. He was her rock. His powerful presence was all the strength Tina needed.

She leaned into him, allowing her emotions free rein.

Tears mixed with the steamy water from Mike's shower-soaked T-shirt.

He simply stood there, murmuring soft words against her head. "I've got you, sweetheart… I've got you."

Chapter Twenty-Five

Mike sat behind the wheel of his motorhome, en route to Townsend, Tennessee to pay a visit to Renee Ransom's seventy-five-year-old mother.

According to the records he'd managed to dig up, Ruth Updike had never remarried after her husband's death some ten years ago.

The small town of Townsend, population four hundred and forty-eight souls, had been Ruth's home since her early thirties.

Birth records showed that Renee had been born in Tennessee as well before moving to Alabama with a classmate to attend Troy State University. Which was where she'd obviously met Levi, since his hometown had been Selma, Alabama.

Tina suddenly appeared in the rearview mirror, coming up the aisle. She placed a soda in Mike's cupholder and lowered herself into the passenger seat. "Where are we?"

"Almost to the campground. How are you feeling?"

She turned her head in his direction. "What did I do to deserve you?"

"I was just thinking the same thing about you."

"Liar," she teased, opening her own soda. She took a sip, wiping at her mouth with the back of her hand. "Thank you for doing this. Seriously."

Mike brushed off her praise. "I just hope we're not about to dredge up painful memories for the mother."

"Me too," Tina softly admitted. "But digging into Renee's past could very well uncover some things about Levi that might help the FBI locate him."

Mike agreed. "I know. And that's the only reason I'm doing this. I don't feel good about it. I just want to put the hitcher behind us for good."

Tina slowly faced him again. "The hitcher?"

"That's what the media has dubbed him. Since…"

"Since people are dumb enough to pick him up," Tina finished, after Mike's words simply trailed off.

Mike shook his head. "That's not what I meant, sweetheart."

"I know. But it's true. I gave him a ride, same as Gary Rowland, and God knows who else that we're unaware of."

The campground came into view, saving Mike from having to respond. He hated that Tina blamed herself for what had happened to Roslynn. But victims always tended to take the blame.

Mike figured it to be all the "what-ifs" that no doubt plagued their tortured minds. But it killed him to think of Tina being tortured. He wanted her happy and whole, free of the torment of Levi Ransom... Free of the hitcher.

He turned into the campground, left the motorhome running, and opened his door. "I'm going to run in and take care of the paperwork. I'll be back shortly."

Tina nodded before shifting her gaze to the side window.

Jumping to the ground, Mike closed his door and hurried around to the building labeled OFFICE.

Once he had them checked in to their spot, he and Tina would sit down and go over the plan. They would need to be on the same page when approaching Renee's mother.

* * * *

Mike drove his car up the gravel road leading to Ruth Updike's address.

Tina hadn't said much on the short drive to Townsend, her mind no doubt a myriad of emotions. Mike could see them playing across her face.

"It's going to be okay, baby. You don't have to say anything. I'll do all the talking."

Tina shifted in her seat. "I'm fine. I was just thinking about Ruth and her reaction to our visit. I'm sure it won't be a good one."

"You're probably right. But we're here now."

A small, pale blue house came into view, on the right side boasting a white porch that held a swing.

The yard appeared neat and freshly mowed, with flower beds in bloom around the house.

A child's swing set sat off to the left under a giant tree, along with a few toy trucks.

Parked under a carport off to the right of the house was a beige-colored station wagon that looked to be about ten years old.

Mike glanced at Tina. "That's odd."

"What is?"

"The toys. The swing set. I wasn't aware that Ruth had any children other than Renee."

Coming to a stop, Mike put the car in park, got out, and hurried around to open Tina's door.

"Maybe she has nieces and nephews," Tina continued, allowing Mike to help her out.

Taking Tina by the hand, Mike strolled up the walkway, mindful of keeping his pace slow. Though she tried to act as if she were fine, he knew her leg still pained her.

The two of them made their way up the steps to the porch.

Mike rang the bell.

A television muted inside the house, and the door opened a moment later.

An older woman stood in the doorway, her gray hair pulled back into a tidy bun, and her fingers holding the top of her rose-colored robe together. "Can I help you?"

"Are you Ruth Updike?" Mike asked in a gentle tone.

The woman nodded. "I am. And you are?"

Mike extended his hand. "I'm Mike Parker, and this is Tina Duggar."

Ruth staggered back a step, her hand flying to her throat. She stared at Tina as if she were the Devil himself. "What do you want?"

Mike lowered his outstretched hand, placing most of his body protectively in front of Tina. "We just need to ask you a few questions. We won't keep you long."

"Questions about what?" Ruth wheezed, attempting to see around Mike.

Mike looked her straight in the eye. "Your daughter, Renee."

Ruth backed up another step, clenching her robe more firmly around her neck. She grabbed onto the door in an attempt to close it.

"Wait," Tina pleaded, stepping out from behind Mike. "It's obvious you've heard of me. Which means you know why I've come. Levi Ransom has killed someone very dear to me. He tried to kill me as well. He's still out there, Miss Updike. Free to hurt someone else. We just want a little information. That's all. No one will know we were here."

The older woman stared back at Tina for so long Mike was sure she would shut that door in Tina's face. But she didn't.

Backing up a step, Ruth conceded. "Come in."

Chapter Twenty-Six

Tina stepped over the threshold of Ruth Updike's cozy home, immediately noticing the absence of pictures on the walls. Not one single photo of Renee appeared in the room. *How strange.*

"Have a seat," Ruth offered, waving a hand toward a brown leather sofa.

Mike took hold of Tina's hand once more, sat, and then tugged her down next to him.

It wasn't lost on Tina that he'd seated himself closest to Ruth. Tina knew it was his way of unconsciously protecting her from the elderly woman. Though she had no idea why.

Ruth cleared her throat and met Tina's gaze. "I'm sorry about what happened to you. And you're right about that boy. He will hurt someone else. Which is why I want you to ask your questions and then leave. If he somehow finds out that you were here…"

"He won't," Tina quickly assured her. "No one knows we've come. We didn't tell anyone."

Ruth didn't look convinced. "I knew Levi was evil the minute Renee brought him home to introduce him to me. How she couldn't see it is beyond me. It was evident in his eyes."

She shifted in her seat and continued. "He knew that I saw through him, too. I tried to talk some sense into Renee, but he had some kind of hold on her. She wouldn't listen to me."

"What happened?" Tina pressed when Ruth grew quiet.

"They left. She went back to Alabama with him, dropped out of school, and married him."

That surprised Tina. Although it shouldn't have. She'd seen Levi in action with Roslynn, knew how convincing he could be. "What made Renee decide to leave him?"

Ruth began to fidget, picking at her fingernails and wringing her hands. "She said he'd started coming home late, at least three nights a week. A couple times, she found blood on his clothes. When she confronted him about it, he tied her to a chair and held a knife to her throat. Threatened to kill her if she spoke of it to anyone. He held her there all night until she urinated on herself." Her voice broke on that last sentence.

"She was headed here to get away from him when the accident happened?" Tina gently asked, sitting forward to better see around Mike's shoulder.

Ruth only nodded. No tears, no sadness reflecting from her eyes. Only a calm sense of satisfaction.

"How far along in her pregnancy was she?" Tina wasn't sure why she brought up the pregnancy. But she wanted any and all information she could gather.

Ruth's face turned ghost white. "Who told you about her baby?"

"Levi confessed it while holding a knife to my throat. He said I reminded him of her."

Suddenly standing, Ruth gestured toward the door. "I'm going to have to insist that you leave now. Please."

Tina stood, as did Mike. She stopped next to Ruth, not knowing what to say, but needing to say something—anything. "I'm sorry about your daughter. Truly, I am."

Ruth didn't respond, simply followed them to the door and waited for them to depart.

Mike and Tina didn't speak until they reached the safety of the car.

"What on earth was that?" Tina questioned the second Mike started the engine.

He put the vehicle in reverse and backed out of the drive. "I'll tell you what that was. Her trying to protect her daughter."

Not fully grasping his meaning, Tina stared at his profile. "What are you talking about?"

"Renee Ransom isn't dead."

"How do you know that?"

Mike straightened the car and pulled out onto the main road. "Four reasons. One, the lack of reaction when you mentioned the car accident. Two, the look on her face when you asked about Renee's pregnancy. Three, she said, *'who told you about her baby?'* Not *pregnancy*, but *baby*. And four, there were no pictures of her daughter displayed anywhere that I could see."

Tina blinked. "I noticed that too. But her using the term *baby* instead of *pregnancy*? What does that have to do with anything?"

Mike shrugged. "Think about it. Had it been you, how would you have answered?"

Tina considered his words. "I guess I would have said, how did you know she'd been pregnant?"

"Exactly."

"So you think Renee staged her own death." It wasn't a question.

Mike drove back toward the campground. "I can't be a hundred percent sure, but it makes sense."

"But why not just disappear, leave the country, change your identity? Isn't staging your death a crime?"

Mike glanced over at her. "Actually, it's not. There is no federal statute that would apply to an individual who fakes their own death."

He returned his attention to the road but continued. "According to missing person search-and-rescue, the right to disappear often causes conflicts between law enforcement and the families of the missing. People think the police should do more to search for their missing family member. But if there's no evidence of foul play involved, the police may not pursue a missing adult."

Tina let that sink in. "But disappearing and having a death certificate filed are two different animals."

"Not really," Mike argued, flipping on his blinker to pass a slow-moving car. "As long as she didn't commit insurance fraud by collecting life insurance or something similar, it's technically not illegal. There's a fine line there, sure, but prosecuting someone for it? Nearly impossible unless fraud is the motive. Otherwise, it's a case of a monumental lie. Nothing more."

Tina ran a hand through her hair. "Faking her death would actually be the smart thing to do. She probably knew that if she tried to disappear, Levi would hunt her to the ends of the earth."

A thought occurred to Tina. "If there's a chance that Renee is actually alive, what do you want to bet those toys belong to the child she was carrying when her car went over that cliff."

Mike practically stood up on the brakes, whipped onto a side road, and turned the car around. "You're right. A hundred bucks says Ruth is getting dressed to go meet her daughter as we speak. At the very least, she's called Renee to warn her of us nosing around, asking questions."

Chapter Twenty-Seven

Mike drove like a speed demon back to Ruth Updike's place. He stopped before turning onto her drive, backed the car into a partial clearing in some nearby woods, and parked. "We'll be able to see from here if she leaves."

Leaving the vehicle running, Mike got out, suggesting Tina not follow. He leaned down far enough inside his open door to see her face. "I'd hate for you to have to run on that leg. I'll be back as soon as she makes a move."

"What if we're wrong?"

Mike shook his head. "We're not."

He closed the door and hurried through the trees to a small hill, where he could see Ruth's house undetected. And prepared to wait.

He didn't have to wait long. Ruth exited her front door, dressed in a pair of blue pants and a cream-colored top.

She ambled around to her station wagon, opened the door, and climbed behind the wheel.

Mike jogged back to his own vehicle to find Tina waiting where he'd left her.

He quickly got in. "She's on the move."

Buckling his seatbelt, he waited for Ruth to turn onto the main road and then followed.

He stayed a good distance behind her to prevent her from noticing him.

"What are we going to do when we find Renee?" Tina softly asked.

Mike shrugged. "Notify the FBI."

Tina's mouth dropped open. "But why? She obviously doesn't want to be found. I know I wouldn't if I were in her position."

Mike answered without hesitation. "If Renee is alive, she would be the perfect tool to draw out the hitcher."

Tina continued to stare at him, her face pale and drawn. "I'm not sure how I feel about that."

"It sounds bad, I know. But if it will help draw out Ransom and possibly prevent him from hurting anyone else, it's worth it in my book."

"What if it were me?" Tina quietly asked. "Would you use me as bait?"

Mike met her gaze before returning his attention to the road. "No, I wouldn't. And I would kill anyone who tried."

Tina turned to look out her window, obviously willing to drop the conversation. For which Mike was grateful. But what he'd said to her was true. He would kill for her. And that scared him more than he wanted to admit.

Ruth's station wagon suddenly took a right onto a clay road.

Mike tapped his brakes, staying back far enough to go unnoticed.

He slowed to a crawl before turning onto the same clay road.

Ruth's taillights flashed, letting Mike know that she would be stopping soon.

"I see a metal roof," Tina announced, leaning forward with her hands clutching the dash. "Through there." She jerked her chin toward the left side of the road.

Mike saw it too.

The station wagon turned up an incline that would lead Ruth to the metal roof seen through the trees.

Mike followed.

"You're just going to pull in right behind her? What if she circles around and leaves?" One of Tina's eyebrows lifted.

Mike shrugged. "It's not her I'm looking for. She's already led us to Renee."

He took the incline as Ruth had, drove up the hill, and stopped behind the station wagon.

Ruth practically jumped out, her face red with rage.

Switching off the car, Mike got out and met Ruth halfway across the yard.

"What do you think you are doing?" Ruth spat without preamble.

Mike held up both hands, a move meant to defuse confrontation. "We know that your daughter is alive, Miss Updike. I just want to talk to her."

Ruth began to cry, which tore at Mike's heart. He tried to harden himself against her tears, to no avail.

Lowering his arms, he dragged a hand down his face. "Look, Miss Updike. I didn't come here to cause trouble or upset you. I—"

"Then why did you come?" a dark-haired woman bit out, suddenly standing in the doorway of the house, a pistol aimed in Mike's direction.

It bothered Mike that he hadn't noticed the door opening, so caught up was he in the elderly woman crying in front of him.

He lifted his arms out to his sides once more. "Renee? Renee Ransom?"

She stepped onto the porch, her eyes narrowed, and that gun held in a surprisingly steady grip. "Renee's dead. Been dead for years."

Tina abruptly appeared at Mike's side, her gaze locked on the woman standing on that porch. "Levi hurt me too."

Reaching up and laying her finger beneath her eye, Tina dragged the tip along the red scar on her cheek. "But it's the inner scars that never heal. Isn't that right, Renee?"

The woman on the porch lowered the pistol, defeat evident in her stance.

Mike could see the resignation in her eyes, along with tears.

"Come on," was all Renee said before spinning around and entering the house.

Chapter Twenty-Eight

Tina walked beside Mike to the porch of a white, wood-framed house sitting on one of the most gorgeous pieces of land she'd ever seen.

The trees alone were enough to take Tina's breath. She loved the outdoors. Always had.

Flowers coupled with ferns hung from the porch on all sides. Everything seemed shaded and cared for.

Loved, Tina thought, stepping up onto said porch. The woman known as Renee *loved* her home. And it showed.

Tina stood back, allowing a stiff-shouldered Ruth to enter ahead of her. She then followed the elderly woman inside, with Mike bringing up the rear.

He shut the door the second they all cleared the threshold.

The dark-haired woman came from the hallway and stepped into the room, her hands empty of weapons. Apparently, she'd put the gun away.

Tina immediately recognized her from the photo she'd seen in the online article. The woman's hair appeared different, but the face belonged to Renee.

"So, you found me," Renee began, gesturing for everyone to sit.

Ruth hurried to her daughter's side. "I'm so sorry, honey. I had no idea they would lie in wait for me."

"It's okay, Mama. I always wondered if this day would come."

After helping her mother sit, Renee joined her on a small loveseat and then met Tina's gaze. "Levi did that?"

Tina lifted her fingers to the scar once again. "Among other things. I was one of the lucky ones who managed to escape."

Renee blinked rapidly, obviously attempting to hold back her tears. "How do you know Levi?"

"I don't," Tina softly admitted. "I was unfortunate enough to give him a ride after his car broke down. I paid dearly for it."

Renee began scrubbing her palms along the front of her jeans. She opened her mouth to speak, but stopped when a boy about five years old came running through the house, holding a toy car in his hand.

"Mama?" he questioned, coming up short. His gaze touched on everyone in the room before settling on Ruth. "Grandma!"

Tina watched him dart across the carpet to stand between Ruth's knees.

Renee sent the boy a smile. "Raymond? Why don't you show Grandma your new playhouse?"

Raymond took Ruth by the hand. "Come on, Grandma. You'll love it."

Ruth got to her feet. She kept hold of Raymond's hand and allowed him to lead her from the room. The sound of a door closed in the distance.

Renee blew out a breath. "I don't want him knowing anything."

"I understand," Tina sent back. "Is he Levi's son?"

Renee's eyes turned red with unshed tears. "He's mine. That monster is just the sperm donor."

Compassion filled Tina's heart. "Tell me what happened to you."

A long pause ensued. And then, "I loved Levi. Loved him so much I couldn't see the demon lurking beneath the surface."

Taking a deep breath, Renee pushed on. "He dictated my every move, controlled how I dressed, who I had dealings with. Until he'd isolated me from everyone I'd ever cared about."

"What happened next?" The question came from Mike.

Renee met his gaze. "I dropped out of school. Levi was so jealous; he couldn't handle me going to college. He began coming home late most nights, acting strange. When I noticed blood on his clothes, I questioned him about it."

"And did he tell you where the blood came from?" Mike gently pressed.

Renee shook her head. "No. But he started becoming violent, the more questions I asked. So, I stopped asking them."

More tears filled her eyes. "He changed when I became pregnant. He hovered over me, doted on me. Things became better for a while. Until one night he didn't come home again."

Mike jumped up, plucked some tissues from a carboard box on a side table, and handed them to her. "What did you do when he didn't come home?"

"I got worried when he wouldn't answer his cell phone, so I called the police, only to be told there was nothing they could do until he'd been missing for over twenty-four hours. He had stayed out late before, but never all night."

Dabbing at her eyes with the tissues, Renee grew still. She gazed across the room as if caught up in a memory she couldn't escape.

"He came home around five that following morning. He wasn't wearing a shirt, and he had blood on his pants. When I questioned him about it, he flew into a rage, tied me to a chair, and held a knife to my throat. He kept me there for hours."

She shifted her gaze to Tina. "He wanted to kill me. I could see it in his eyes. He wanted to so much, his hands shook with it, and he began talking to himself."

Tina knew exactly what Renee meant. She herself had experienced the insanity of Levi. "For some reason, he spared you."

Renee blew out a shuddering breath. "I begged him not to hurt me. I *begged*. It wasn't until I pleaded for our unborn child that he stopped. He untied me, made me shower, and then he…"

"He what?" Mike prompted, when her words faded off, and that faraway look returned to her eyes.

Renee opened her mouth but continued to stare off into the distance, new tears leaking from her eyes. "He forced me to have sex with him. He — Some blood was dried on the side of his face. He rubbed it against my cheeks, as if... As if marking me with it."

Tina stood, hurried to Renee's side, and placed her arm around the woman's shoulders.

Renee shuddered against her. "I left as soon as he passed out. I didn't take anything but my purse. No clothes, nothing. I only knew that I had to get away from him. And Mama was all I had."

Tina rubbed her palm along Renee's arm. "So you drove to Tennessee."

"Yes. I didn't think beyond getting away. But the seven-hour drive gave me time to calm down and think. I knew I would never be free of him if I didn't disappear. Never. And my baby..."

Another shudder passed through Renee. "The decision to die didn't come until I reached the mountains. There are cliffs here, high enough that I knew I could send my car over one of them, and no one would know about it for days, possibly weeks. Which meant that if my body was never found, no one would question it. Not with the wild animals that live in these mountains."

Renee seemed to calm somewhat, relieving Tina of having to comfort her.

Tina returned to her position next to Mike. "What did you do once you decided to disappear?"

"I called Mama and had her meet me near the steepest point I knew of. When she arrived, I left the car running, put it in drive, and got out. It idled itself over the cliff. I left my phone, purse, everything inside, got in the car with Mama, and she took me to a motel. I'm sure you can figure out the rest."

Chapter Twenty-Nine

Mike sat there quietly, listening to Renee's remarkable story of how she'd escaped a serial killer. The lengths she'd gone to in order to save herself and the life of her unborn child were, quite frankly, amazing. "Did Levi look for you?"

Renee lifted her gaze. "What do you think? A man like Levi would walk through Hell to take back what he felt was his. And we *were* his. We belonged to him. His possessions, his…trophies. He would have never let me go any other way. He *had* to think me dead."

Compassion swelled inside Mike's chest. "So, he showed up at your mother's?"

"Yes. Mama told him that I'd called her and told her I would be coming, but that I didn't give her a specific date or time. So, he left to get a room. And do you know where he ended up staying?"

When Mike only lifted his eyebrows, she said, "At the same motel I was staying in."

Mike pinched the bridge of his nose. His stomach had long since gone tight with nervous energy.

There he sat, across from a woman who was supposed to have died six years ago, who now had a son and lived in the mountains, hiding from a serial killer known as the hitcher.

How could Mike possibly inform the FBI of her existence? It wasn't only her life that would be uprooted but Raymond's as well.

He reached up and massaged his temples, fighting against the headache forming behind his eyes. "Go on."

"Mom paid cash for my motel room. She had food delivered to me as often as she could, and I remained inside until my car was found, and the search for my body ended. It was finally determined that I'd died, and my remains likely eaten by animals."

"That's when Levi returned to Alabama?" Mike asked, noticing the look of relief on Renee's face.

"Once he got the official report, he did. And as far as I know, he's never been back. I haven't heard anything from or about him since. Until last week when I saw his face on the news."

"That had to have been terrifying for you," Tina whispered, sitting forward with her forearms resting on her knees.

Renee shifted her attention to Tina. "Not as terrifying as it was for you, I'm sure. But yes, it scared me. Not for myself, but for Raymond. If Levi ever found out that I lived, and that I gave birth to a son, there is nowhere on this planet safe enough for us. He would take my son, Miss Duggar. And he would…kill me."

"No one is going to harm you or your son," Mike assured her, not bothering to glance in Tina's direction. He would find the same look in her eyes that he himself felt. He couldn't inform the FBI that Renee lived. He just couldn't. "How have you stayed beneath the radar? Did you change your name?"

Renee licked her lips. "Yes, I had to for Raymond's sake. He's good, my Raymond. Good to his soul. He wasn't tainted by his father's genes, his demonic mind. He's smart and funny, kind and generous."

A sigh of what sounded like exhaustion left Renee. "After doing a lot of research, I found a man who created birth certificates, social security numbers, and such. It cost Mama nearly half her savings, but she paid for it all. And my name changed from Renee Ransom to—"

Mike held up a hand, stopping her from speaking the words aloud. He pushed to his feet, helping Tina to stand as well. "I don't want to know."

Renee's eyes grew misty again. She stood, her expression radiating uncertainty. "You... Does that mean...?"

"We were never here. We'll find Levi some other way."

Striding to the door, Mike stopped with his hand on the knob. He met Renee's gaze over his shoulder. "I wish you and your son all the best life has to offer. After everything you've been through, you deserve it. You can go to your grave being assured that Tina and I will take this knowledge to ours."

"Thank you," Renee whispered, her hand hovering near her mouth. "Thank you both."

She shifted her gaze to Tina. "I'm glad you escaped that monster."

Mike saw Tina's nod through his peripheral. She stepped in closer to his side. "Me too. We're survivors, you and I. We'll always have that."

Once on the porch, Mike lifted a hand to wave goodbye to Ruth.

He received a middle finger salute in response.

A grin split his lips. He kind of liked Ruth. She was a tough one. Like a hen protecting her chicks.

Well, her chicks were safe. Mike would leave the knowledge of their existence in the mountains of Tennessee. Along with their secrets.

Chapter Thirty

After staying the night at the campground in Tennessee, Tina and Mike departed the mountainous state and drove the seven-hour trek to the small town of Selma, Alabama. The town where Alma Ransom, Levi's mother, resided.

Unlike meeting Ruth Updike, Tina was more than a little nervous about rolling up on the property of Alma Ransom, the mother of a serial killer.

Would she resent Tina or blame her for Levi being on the run?

"Hey." Mike reached across the seat of his car and touched Tina's arm. They'd parked the motorhome at a local truck stop and unhooked Mike's vehicle to drive the five-mile distance to Alma's. "If you're worried about this, you can stay in the car while I talk to her."

Tina shook her head. "I need to meet her. I can't explain why. I just feel that it will shed some light on why her son did the things he did to us."

"You don't ever have to worry about him touching you again, sweetheart. I'll never let that happen. Even if I have to stay by your side twenty-four hours a day."

God, Tina loved Mike. She sent him a lopsided smile. "You can't be with me every second of every day. You have to work. We both do."

"I'm turning in my resignation when we get home."

Tina jerked her head in his direction. "What?"

"With the car dealerships my father left me, not to mention the large sum of money, I'll be able to take an early retirement."

Tina didn't know what to say. On the one hand, she was ecstatic for him that he could retire early, but on the other, she wondered if he would be happy not doing what he loved the most. Investigating. "Are you sure that's what you want to do?"

Mike shrugged. "It'll take some getting used to, but I'm sure I'll manage."

He turned his attention to the GPS on his phone. "We're almost there."

Tina's heart began to pound. "I'm going in with you."

"Are you sure?"

"I am."

Mike slowed at the next drive and carefully maneuvered his car around a large pothole in the road.

Tina could see a small, singlewide trailer up ahead, out in the open with no trees for shade.

The grass needed to be cut, and an old, gray car was parked out front.

They stopped behind the car, both exiting their vehicle.

A noise, low and pitiful sounding, came from somewhere in front of the car.

Tina glanced at Mike, who had already moved in the direction of the sound.

She followed close behind. What she saw there nearly ripped her heart in half.

A skeleton of a dog stared up at her, its ribs prominent along its back. The animal had been tied to the bumper of the car, unable to reach its food and water dishes. Which were both empty.

Rage flew through Tina at the cruelty the dog had to have endured.

Without thought to the woman who lived there, Tina snatched up one of the empty bowls, filled it from a faucet at the corner of the trailer, and carried it to the dog's side.

The dog could barely stand but managed to get to its feet and lap thirstily at the water.

"What are y'all doin' over there?" a woman demanded from somewhere to Tina's right.

Tina looked up in time to see a woman standing in the open doorway of the trailer, her faded blonde hair a rat's nest on her head. She wore a stained-up smock, no shoes, and had a cigarette burning between her fingers.

Still in a rage over the shape of that poor dog, Tina marched in her direction. "Do you have any food for your dog?"

The woman squinted her eyes. "He's out. Ain't had a ride to the store in days."

"So, he hasn't eaten in days?" Tina asked incredulously, attempting to rein in her temper. It didn't work. "He's about to die."

The woman sighed and then took a draw from her cigarette. "What is it that y'all want?"

Mike touched Tina on the small of her back. She hadn't even heard him approach.

He stepped around her and headed toward the trailer steps. "Are you Alma Ransom?"

"Who wants to know?"

Mike cleared his throat. "We'd like to ask you some questions about your son."

"I've done told the cops all I know. FBI was out here too. Told them the same as I told them cops. I ain't seen Levi in years. He ran off chasin' some tail, not carin' two hoots if his mama starved to death or not."

Tina glanced back at the dog still lapping up that water. Levi obviously came by his sickness honestly. Alma could give two hoots if her dog starved to death either.

"We're not here to ask the kind of questions you got from the FBI," Mike calmly pointed out. "We're here for a different reason."

Alma took another drag from her cigarette, flicked it into the yard, and waved them forward. "Come on then."

Chapter Thirty-One

Mike took the metal steps that led inside the trailer. Heat blasted him in the face, along with the stench of garbage and stale cigarette smoke.

He waited for Tina to enter behind him and then moved to stand along the wall next to the open door, where he could somewhat breathe.

Alma took a seat in a well-worn recliner, and, of course, lit another cigarette. "Sit down if you want."

"That's okay," Mike politely declined. "We'll stand."

"Suit yourself. What is it you wanna know?"

Mike clasped his hands in front of him, a move he knew would make him appear less threatening. "My name is Mike Parker." He nodded in Tina's direction. "This is Tina Duggar, one of the victims who survived Levi."

Alma's eyes widened. She drew on that cigarette until the red cherry on the end threatened to drop in her lap.

Exhaling the smoke, she murmured, "You here to tell me how twisted Levi is? All the bad stuff he's done? Well, you're preachin' to the choir. I already know all about him."

Mike noticed Tina hug her waist. He could feel her emotions as if they were his own.

Tina asked, "Was Levi always disturbed?"

"Disturbed?" Alma mockingly laughed. "He was more than disturbed. I caught him hurtin' animals when he weren't no more than five years old. Spankin' him didn't do no good, only made him harder, angrier."

Mike moved closer to Tina's side, careful not to brush against the nicotine-stained wall. He kept his gaze on Alma. "Did he have any friends growing up?"

"He had a few, but they didn't hang around long. Levi kept 'em all in trouble at school, so their parents changed their classes and wouldn't let 'em come over no more."

Mike pulled out a pen and small pad from his shirt pocket. "You wouldn't happen to recall their names, would you?"

"Are you kiddin' me? That's been nigh of thirty years. I don't even remember the name of the school anymore."

Tina shifted to her other foot, her arm brushing against Mike's. "What about Levi's father?"

"He left when Levi was about six years old. Ain't heard from him since. Sorry is what he is. Left us with nothin' but a car that wouldn't run half the time and this dump of a trailer. Never paid no child support or sent so much as a birthday card for his boy."

"So, you have no idea where Levi might be?" Tina quietly asked. "Did he have a favorite place he liked to go to?"

Alma snuffed out her cigarette in an overflowing ashtray next to her chair. "Like I told the police and them agents, I ain't seen or heard from Levi in years. Y'all wasted your time comin' here."

Mike took Tina by the elbow, sent Alma a nod, and then turned toward the door. "We appreciate you taking the time to speak with us."

Tina dug in her heels before descending the steps. "How much will you take for the dog?"

Alma's eyes lit up. "What you want with that ole mutt?"

Mike could feel the anger radiating from Tina. She reached into the pocket of her jeans and pulled out two twenty-dollar bills. "I'll give you forty bucks for him."

Alma was out of that chair and snatching up the money in an instant. "Deal."

Mike followed Tina down the steps and back to the dog tied to the bumper of that old car.

Tina quickly untied him. "Come on, boy."

She scooped the skinny dog up and marched toward Mike's car.

Mike hurried ahead to open her door.

Tina shook her head. "I'll sit in the back with him until we get to the RV."

Once Tina and the dog were seated, Mike shut her door and rounded the car to climb behind the wheel. "What are you going to do with him?"

"I don't know yet, but I couldn't leave him there. I just couldn't."

The enormous amount of love Mike carried in his heart for Tina paled in comparison to what he felt for her in that moment.

She had the kindest, most giving soul he'd ever known. And she was his.

Chapter Thirty-Two

Tina fought tears as she gazed down into the leery eyes of the dog in her lap.

He stared straight ahead, his body trembling, as if afraid she would hurt him somehow.

With slow movements, she brought her hand to his head and gently dragged her palm down his neck. "You're a good boy, aren't you? You're safe now... No one will ever hurt you again."

The car came to a stop next to the motorhome. Tina had been so wrapped up in the malnourished dog in her lap, she hadn't paid attention to the drive.

Mike got out and opened her door. "Want me to take him?"

Tina shook her head. "He's terrified. I'll carry him."

Mike hurried ahead, unlocked the RV, and helped Tina enter. He then started the engine, switched on the air conditioning, and filled a bowl with water.

Tina grabbed a blanket from a small closet in the hall and situated it near the water bowl. "Take us home, Mike."

"Yes, ma'am." Mike kissed her on the forehead. "I'm going to hook up the car. I'll be back shortly."

Tina set down the dog who, of course, went straight for the water bowl. "Okay."

She grabbed another dish, opened the refrigerator, and plucked up the first thing she saw. A pack of hotdogs.

Opening the pack, she broke the hotdogs in pieces, placed them in the dish, and then set it next to the pitiful-looking creature still lapping up that water.

He tore into the food, scarfing it down in less than a minute.

Tina's heart felt as if it ripped in half.

She went back to the refrigerator, this time taking out a couple packs of ham. Those also went into the dish and, of course, were eaten without being chewed.

Mike reentered the motorhome and eased them out of the truck stop parking lot.

Tina slowly lowered herself to the floor next to the poor dog. "Was that good, Buddy?"

She realized she'd just given the dog a name. "Buddy. I like it. It just...fits you."

Once Buddy helped himself to more water, he raised his head and eyed Tina.

She slowly patted the blanket she'd put down for him. "Come on, Buddy. It's okay. You can lie down and sleep if you want."

Buddy, of course, had other ideas. He moved away, his body still in that bowed position, his tail tucked between his legs. Tina's heart ached. His tan fur should be shiny and soft, not dull and scarred.

"Okay, I'll leave you be so you can snoop around." Pushing to her feet, Tina made her way to the front to sit in the passenger seat.

Mike sent her a smile. "How's he doing?"

"He ate just about everything we had in the fridge. God knows how long it's been since he's eaten. I named him Buddy."

Mike's eyebrows lifted. "Since you named him, that must mean you're planning on keeping him."

"Yes," Tina admitted, realizing that she'd decided to keep Buddy the moment she'd laid eyes on him. "I'll take him to the vet as soon as we get home. Have him checked out."

She opened her mouth to continue but noticed a suspicious moisture in Mike's eyes. "What is it?"

"Nothing," he quietly responded, glancing in her direction. "I..."

He suddenly slowed the RV and pulled over on the side of the road.

Tina watched in surprise as Mike removed his seatbelt, opened a compartment near the steering wheel, and removed a small, black box.

"I was going to do this when we got home, but I don't think I can wait."

Tina's heart began to pound. An incredible amount of love for this man exploded inside her. She stared in wonder as he opened the box, pulled a beautiful diamond ring from its depths, and then lowered to one knee between their seats.

He took hold of her trembling left hand. "I have loved you since the moment you entered my life, with your infectious smile and your incredible eyes. You're not just beautiful, Tina, you're gorgeous on the inside as well. And I want you by my side for the rest of my life. Tina Duggar, will you marry me?"

Tina couldn't speak. She could only stare down into Mike's mesmerizing, hazel-colored eyes and see her future reflected there.

"Tina?"

"Yes," she breathed, realizing that tears leaked from her eyes. "A thousand times, yes!"

He slipped that gorgeous ring onto her finger, sealing their engagement.

Tina held her hand up to the light, watching the diamond sparkle through her tears. "It's beautiful, Mike."

"You're beautiful," he confessed, bringing her gaze back to him.

She threw her arms around his neck. "I love you so much."

"Not as much as I love you."

Something nudged Tina's leg. She pulled back to see Buddy sitting next to her, touching his nose to her thigh.

"He likes you," Mike pointed out, laughter in his voice. He kissed Tina softly on the lips and then returned to his seat.

Tina rubbed the top of Buddy's head. "I like you too, boy."

Though insecurity still lingered in Buddy's eyes, a spark of trust could be seen there as well.

After everything Tina had endured at the hands of Levi Ransom, she had come out the other side, alive. Alive and…loved.

Chapter Thirty-Three

Mike sat in his home office, staring at the cell phone in his hand. He'd gotten a call from Sheriff Mulligan.

Two more bodies had been stabbed to death in Florida and dumped on the side of Interstate 10. Which meant that the hitcher was still in the area.

"Is everything all right?"

Mike looked up into Tina's concerned eyes. She had been staying with him since her accident. And now that they'd become engaged, the two of them had plans to move into the house Mike's father had left him.

Mike thought about not telling her about the hitcher, but that wouldn't be fair to her. As much as he hated upsetting her, she needed to remain vigilant until that monster was caught.

"Two more bodies were discovered while we were gone."

"What? Where?" Tina stepped into the room.

"At two sperate locations along Interstate 10."

Her face paled. "He-he's still in Florida." It wasn't a question. "Are they sure it's him?"

"Fingerprints were found at the scene. Both places."

Mike could see the fear in Tina's eyes. And it killed him inside that she should have to live that way. "They'll catch him, baby. I promise."

Tina absently nodded, moving to stand in front of the window. "I try to imagine what it's like to be inside his mind. How a person like Levi thinks. The need to kill, to torment, and enjoy another person's fear."

"You can't figure out illogic with logic, Tina. It'll only drive you nuts."

She continued to stand there, looking through the blinds. "I wonder if something happened to him in his childhood that made him this way. Or if he was simply born without empathy."

Mike pushed to his feet and moved to stand behind her. He encircled her in his arms, resting his chin on top of her head. "That's something we may never know. But from meeting his mother, I'd say there's a good chance he suffered abuse."

"Like Buddy did."

"Yes," Mike agreed, thinking about the dog Tina had rescued. "Speaking of, where is he?"

"In our bed," Tina answered with a laugh.

Mike's lips twitched. "You know that's not going to work, right?"

"Says who?" More laughter.

"Says who, indeed."

She turned in his arms. "Buddy has a long road ahead of him. He had every kind of worm you could imagine. Including heartworms."

"I know." Mike hugged her tighter. "But the medication will rid him of it all. He'll be good to go pretty soon."

"A year. It takes a year to slow-kill heartworms." Tina sighed against Mike's neck. "Just imagine if we hadn't gone to Alabama. Buddy would have died out there in the heat. If not from starvation... Or from heartworms."

She pulled back enough to make eye contact. "Do you think serial killers have certain genes that can be passed down to their children?"

Mike shrugged. "Some researchers say yes. But I don't think there's any hard evidence to back up that theory. Why?"

"I was just thinking about Raymond. I pray to God he didn't inherit any of his father's traits."

Mike prayed the same thing. "He looked to be a normal, happy kid to me. As long as his mother keeps him sheltered from his father's stigma, I believe he'll be fine."

"Besides," Mike continued, "you heard what Alma Ransom said. Levi was showing signs of being disturbed when he was a small child. Raymond appeared to be well rounded to me."

Tina nodded. "I'm glad we decided to leave Renee dead. She deserves to be able to live her life and raise her son without fear of Levi finding them."

"Agreed," Mike murmured, releasing his hold on Tina. "I need to make a store run. We can swing by my dad's house on the way if you'd like."

Tina's eyes lit up. "I would love to."

Mike's chest filled with pride. Though it didn't matter to him where they lived as long as they were together, he knew Tina would love the place. And the yard being fenced in would make a perfect place for Buddy to run and enjoy the outdoors.

Taking hold of Tina's hand, Mike led her from the office and out to the car. He helped her inside and then moved around to the driver's seat.

It took less than fifteen minutes to reach the house. Mike glanced over to find Tina staring in amazement.

"It's gorgeous," she breathed, already reaching for the door handle.

The corner of Mike's mouth lifted. "I thought you would like it."

"This isn't where you lived as a child though, is it?"

Mike shook his head. "Not even close. Dad didn't get into the car business until after he and Mom divorced. I didn't see him much after that."

Tina met his gaze. "I'm really sorry, Mike. I couldn't imagine not having my dad around growing up."

"You would make a great mother," Mike admitted, studying the emotions skating across her face.

Tina grew serious. "We've talked about this."

Mike sent her a reassuring smile. "I know. And I'm completely okay with us not having children. I kind of enjoy it being just the two of us. And Buddy," he added with a chuckle.

"And whatever else we adopt along the way."

Mike honestly didn't care if they adopted half the animals in every shelter in the

Panhandle. As long as it made Tina happy. "Whatever you want, babe."

She opened her door. "Let's go see our dream home"

Chapter Thirty-Four

Tina knew her mouth hung open. She didn't care. The house was breathtaking. "Oh, Mike…"

He stepped up next to her. "I take it you like?"

"What's not to like? I love it. It's so open and airy. How many bedrooms does it have?"

"Four. And three bathrooms."

Tina moved from room to room, taking in the sheer beauty of the place.

She came to a set of French doors, unlocked them, and pushed them open. Her breath caught.

The backyard was lined with a privacy fence at least six feet tall. A kidney-shaped swimming pool sat off the patio, surrounded by sago palms.

The grass was green and luscious, giving life to several flower beds scattered about. A birdbath sat off to the left, directly in front of a large oak tree.

"It's perfect, Mike. Buddy is going to love it."

"But will you?" Mike asked, smiling down at her.

Tina lifted an eyebrow. "I think my reaction speaks for itself."

"I'm glad. We don't have to wait for the wedding to move in if you want. We can get started tomorrow."

Tina gazed around at the scene in front of her. "I'd like that. It'll give me time to get settled before I go back to work."

A shadow passed through Mike's eyes. "You don't have to work if you don't want to. We have more than enough money to support us."

Tina understood that Mike didn't want her out of his sight. But she loved her job, loved helping the animals.

"Just think about it," he suggested before she could respond. "You have time."

Not wanting to upset him in any way, Tina merely nodded.

Mike turned back toward the French doors. "Let's go grab some groceries. Tomorrow, we can get started on the move. I have to go to the station at some point to fill Desiree in on the cases I've been working on. She'll be handling my load until my replacement is found."

Tina followed Mike inside and waited while he locked the doors. The two of them left by way of the front entrance, locked that door as well, and then departed to the grocery store.

* * * *

"How long will you be gone?" Tina watched Mike return his cell phone to the clip on his belt and open the front door.

The two of them had slept in that morning, which put Mike behind schedule. He'd driven Tina to a local U-Haul store to buy a few boxes before dropping her at her small house to get started on packing up some things.

"I shouldn't be more than a couple of hours. I have a deputy out front to keep an eye on things while I'm gone."

Tina stepped forward to see around Mike. An unmarked car sat along the side of her drive, a dark-haired man perched behind the wheel.

As much as she hated for the deputy to have to spend his day babysitting her, she was grateful to see him there.

The hitcher hadn't been caught. And from the recent bodies found on the interstate, he was likely still in Florida.

"Will you take him a soda on your way out? I hate that he has to sit in the heat until you get back."

Mike nodded, grabbed a soda from the refrigerator, and returned to the open door. "He's parked in the shade."

"Hopefully, he has air conditioning."

Mike stepped out onto the porch. "He does, but if his windows are up, he can't hear if something happens. He'll be fine, babe. And I'll be back before it gets stupid hot."

Tina kissed Mike goodbye before closing and locking the door.

She pulled her hair back into a ponytail, picked up a box, and made her way into her bedroom. That was where most of her clutter happened to be. She would box up what she wanted, and the rest would be tossed into the trash.

Approaching the dresser, Tina picked up a stack of books resting there and set them on the foot of her bed to go through momentarily.

She turned back to the dresser to find an old picture of Roslynn, Bobbi, and herself, the frame covered in dust.

Tina swiped her palm across the frame's glass, a lump quickly forming in her throat. The picture had been taken at Bobbi's wedding reception.

"Oh, Roz... I'm so sorry." A tear splashed onto the glass.

Memories of Roslynn begging for her life overtook Tina. She remembered every detail of every sound. The muffled screams, gags, groans. The sickening, disgusting grunts that Levi made.

Tina's jaws watered up with nausea.

She would never forget the torment that Roslynn endured, her last hours on earth.

Bringing the frame to her lips, Tina kissed Roslynn's smiling face and then carefully placed it inside the box next to her hip. "Goodbye, my friend…"

Chapter Thirty-Five

Mike arrived at the station approximately ten minutes after leaving Tina's place.

Sheriff Mulligan met him in the parking lot. "Don't leave before I get back. I shouldn't be gone but about an hour."

"Sure thing, Sheriff."

Mulligan clapped Mike on the back and strode off in the direction of his car.

Mike used his keycard to open the back door to the station and then stepped inside.

He trailed off to his office, a feeling of melancholy settling in his chest.

Mike had spent the past twenty years working for the Bay County Sheriff's Office, after hiring on right out of high school. Leaving would definitely be bittersweet.

A sigh escaped him. He sat behind his desk, gazing around at all his accomplishments. He would miss this place. Of that, he had no doubt.

But life with Tina was Mike's dream, where his heart resided. At forty years old, Mike had never married. Never wanted to. Until Tina. And to think he'd almost lost her.

His jaw tightened with the memory of seeing her lying in the recovery room in that hospital. Her face covered in bruises...cuts.

And the monster responsible for it was still at large.

Desiree poked her head around the corner. "Welcome back."

Mike sent her a lopsided smile. "I'm not staying. I've just come to tie up some loose ends."

"I heard you were retiring early. What's going on?" She stepped into the room.

Mike waved her toward the chair in front of his desk.

Once she was seated, he explained the situation with the car dealerships. "It's a big responsibility. One that I can't shirk. Unless I decide to sell them."

"I'm sorry about your dad. He must have loved you very much. You're set for life."

Amidst the resentment Mike normally carried around for his father, a spark of forgiveness was born. His father had left him everything. The man must have loved his son on some level.

But Mike wasn't ready to talk about it. Especially not at the moment, with so much uncertainty going on in his life. "Any news about the hitcher?"

Desiree shook her head. "Not since those latest bodies were discovered on the interstate.

He's ballsy, I'll give him that. A nationwide manhunt is underway and he's still in Florida."

That had struck Mike as strange also. "It's like he's taunting us, laughing at us."

"I know," Desiree readily agreed. "I mean, one would think he would go underground for a while, let things die down before he started killing again. But he hasn't slowed down any at all."

Mike picked up a pen and twirled it through his fingers. "He picked the easiest hunting grounds he could find. With Florida being a tourist state, it's like a buffet for someone like him. Especially during the summer, new people arriving every day."

"How is Tina holding up?"

Mike thought about the trip they'd taken to Tennessee and their stop to speak with Levi's mother in Alabama. The proposal…

"She's getting stronger and healing more with every day that passes. She's taking Roslynn's death pretty hard. Though she tries to hide it from me. I can see it in her eyes when she doesn't think I'm looking."

Desiree leaned back in her chair. "I can imagine. They were friends for a long time. What about the other friend that was with them? I can't remember her name."

"Bobbi?" Mike stared down at that pen he still held. "From what Tina has told me, she's doing as well as can be expected. I know the FBI went to her home to take a statement."

"I didn't know anything about that."

Mike shrugged. "That's what I was told. And with Bobbi being on bedrest, I reckon it makes sense."

"Bedrest?"

"You know she's pregnant, right?"

Desiree nodded. "Yes, of course. But I hadn't heard she'd been put on bedrest. Is everything okay with the baby?"

"I sure hope so."

A light tap on the door brought Mike's gaze up.

"You got a minute?" The sheriff stuck his head inside. "Oh, I'm sorry. I didn't realize you were busy."

Desiree got to her feet. "It's okay, sir. I was just leaving."

The sheriff stepped into the room, nodded to Desiree, and then took up her previous position in the chair.

"I thought you were leaving," Mike commented while the sheriff removed his hat.

Mulligan pulled a handkerchief from his back pocket and wiped at his forehead with it. "I had something to take care of. Didn't take as long as I thought it would."

After a brief pause, Mulligan stated, "We're going to keep eyes on Tina at all times. We'll switch out with a fresh man at every shift. Even when she's with you, I think it best to keep a deputy close by."

Mike couldn't agree more. "Do you think there's a chance this sicko will attempt to get to her?"

"I don't know," the sheriff admitted. "Better to be safe than sorry."

Mike gripped the back of his neck to knead away the tension rising there.

"The FBI has also recommended we put a man on the Deloach place," the sheriff announced. "I sent a deputy to keep an eye on them until this hitcher is caught."

"Good idea." Mike sat forward. "I know I didn't give you a lot of notice about retiring, and I'm sorry for that. But given the circumstances, I may leave even sooner than anticipated."

Since the sheriff already knew of the house and car dealerships Mike's father had left him, Mike didn't have to explain the situation in detail. He simply stated, "There's a lot that has to be done still. Plus, I'm not comfortable leaving Tina alone just yet. In fact, today is the first time since the accident we've been apart."

The murmuring of voices could be heard out in the hall.

Mike glanced toward the door. "What's going on out there?"

"I don't know." The sheriff stood as did Mike.

Mike followed him into the hall to find Desiree moving in their direction, holding some papers in her hand.

She glanced at Mike and then the sheriff. "We just got a fax from the sheriff's office in Marianna. Another body was discovered in their county. A thirty-seven-year-old female, found in her car near the interstate."

"Do they believe the hitcher is responsible?" the sheriff asked, anger lining his voice.

Desiree's expression didn't change. "When I called, they said they couldn't be sure until they finish processing the scene. But it's the same MO. The victim was found nude and stabbed to death. They have a team out there now. They sent a fax over with everything they know so far."

She handed the papers to the sheriff.

Marianna was only an hour from Panama City, which meant the hitcher could still be close by.

"Any road checks in Marianna?" Mike asked Desiree. "Hopefully, he's still in the area."

She sent him a brief nod. "That's what I was told."

"Follow me," Mulligan muttered, already striding off toward his office. "Let's find out what the FBI says."

Chapter Thirty-Six

Tina stepped out of the shower and dressed in a comfortable tank top and some cotton shorts. She blow-dried her hair and then slipped her feet into her favorite pair of flip-flops.

Her new cell phone buzzed on the counter next to the bathroom sink. Since her previous cell phone had been destroyed, she'd lost all her contact's numbers. But she would recognize Bobbi's digits in her sleep.

She plucked the phone up and brought it to her ear. "Hey, you."

"Hey back," Bobbi softly greeted.

Tina trailed to her bedroom to sit on the foot of the bed. A sadness that couldn't be denied lined Bobbi's voice. "How are you holding up?"

"I was about to ask you the same thing."

Tina cleared her throat. "I'm okay. It's hard sometimes to push my way through it. But I have to. How's the baby?"

"The baby is doing good. I'm still on bedrest but hopefully not for much longer. I can't stop thinking about her, Tina."

Tina knew exactly who Bobbi referred to. Roslynn… "Neither can I. Every day, I wake up and forget she's gone. And then the memories return."

A sniffling sound came through the line, telling Tina that Bobbi cried.

"I can still hear her, Tina. Her cries are in my head, every waking minute of every day."

Tina blinked back her own tears. "I do too, Bobbi. I don't know if we'll ever be able to forget."

Bobbi sniffed again. "I miss her so much. To know that I'll never be able to pick up the phone and call her, to hear her silly laugh or eat her horrible cooking. I just can't believe that she's gone."

"I found a picture of the three of us at your wedding reception," Tina revealed. "She looked so happy and beautiful."

More soft crying came through the line. "He killed her, Tina. He really killed her."

"I know, Bobbi," Tina whispered, fighting her own breakdown. "I wish I could go back in time and take back that entire weekend. But I can't. Neither of us can."

Bobbi's shuddering breath echoed in Tina's ear. "Did you hear that he's still out there? Joey said that more bodies have been found on the interstate. In Florida."

Tina had heard. "God knows what else he'll do before they catch him. It's terrifying to imagine all those innocent people traveling, most of them having no idea that a serial killer is even out there. Let alone close by."

"I've been thinking about talking to someone," Bobbi confessed.

"You mean like a psychiatrist?"

"Yeah. Joey thinks it's a good idea as well."

As did Tina. Bobbi didn't sound good at all. "Speaking of Joey, how is he holding up through all this?"

"He's been a Godsend, my rock. He's sober, doting, and caring. I wouldn't have been able to get through this without him."

"I'm glad you have him, Bobbi." Tina wanted to tell Bobbi about her recent engagement to Mike, but she refrained. Now just wasn't the time. This particular phone call needed to be about Bobbi. And Tina wouldn't dare make it about herself.

The two of them talked for a few more minutes before Bobbi had to go.

Tina ended the call, her heart heavy. She understood how Bobbi felt. She herself had trouble dealing with the loss of Roslynn. And Bobbi no doubt was going through hormonal changes. Probably making coping twice as difficult.

Blowing out a despondent breath, Tina left her bedroom and trailed through the living room toward the kitchen.

She noticed the kitchen door standing ajar.

That's odd, she thought, moving closer to the door. Had the deputy opened it to check on her while she showered?

She reached for the knob.

"This is a nice place you have here, Tina."

Tina froze, her heart slamming against her ribs. She would know that voice anywhere.

Her hand fell away. She slowly turned and looked into the manic eyes of Levi Ransom.

Pink scars littered his face, and his left arm sported a bandage. Evidence of the car accident, where Tina had slammed into the power pole on the side of the interstate.

He smiled, showing even, white teeth and eyes that promised retribution. "You've been a bad girl, Tina Duggar."

Tina's gaze lowered to the gun he held. A gun now aimed in her direction.

How had he gotten past the deputy sitting in her drive?

"What do you want?" she whispered, hating the fear that resonated in her voice.

Levi took a step toward her. "You, Tina. I want you. Now, lock the door and go to the other room."

Tina swallowed hard, her terror a living, breathing thing.

She did as he demanded, closing the door and engaging the lock.

"Move!" he barked, sending her scrambling forward.

She could feel him tight on her heels as she progressed to her small dining room on shaky legs.

"Sit."

Tears formed in her eyes against her will. She knew begging would do no good. Not with Levi.

She pulled a chair from beneath the table and took a seat, her mind screaming for the deputy to help her.

"In case you're expecting your friend in the unmarked car to run in here and save you, you can rest easy. He no longer breathes."

Tina didn't have to ask what that meant, but she could no more stop the words from spilling forth than she could stop Levi. "You killed him?"

Levi laughed. "It was really quite easy. He never even saw it coming. Don't worry, he didn't suffer…much."

Bile rose to Tina's throat.

Once he had her where he wanted her, he pulled a roll of duct tape from the waistband of his jeans and moved around behind her.

"Please," she whispered. "Don't."

He finished taping up with her wrists. "Awwww, is Tina crying?"

Her ankles were then secured to the legs of the chair with the duct tape. "There."

Levi straightened and laid the revolver on the table. "You tried to kill me, Tina. You shouldn't have done that."

She opened her mouth to say something—anything—when his fist slammed into her jaw.

Her head snapped back with the force of the blow. Pain exploded inside her skull, and her world turned black.

Chapter Thirty-Seven

"Wakey, wakey."

Tina could feel something tapping on the side of her face, something that added pain to the throbbing in her jaw.

And then, memory invaded her oblivion.

Her eyes rolled around in their sockets in an attempt to open. Finally, Levi's manic face came into focus.

"Ah, there you are," Levi crooned, looming above her.

Tina instinctively shrank back as far as the chair would allow.

He openhandedly slapped her with enough force her head flew to the side.

Tina cried out from the pain and no small amount of fear.

Blood oozed from the corner of her mouth.

Levi disappeared into the kitchen, returning a moment later with a paper towel. He roughly wiped at her bloodied lips.

"You won't get away with this," Tina wheezed through the pain. "The FBI is looking for you."

He propped his knuckles beneath his chin, a stance that made him appear thoughtful. "Ah, yes, the FBI. The federal bureau of idiots. They couldn't catch a fly that had no wings. I hate to say it, love, but you're just fresh out of luck where the FBI are concerned."

"Matter of fact," he continued, shifting his weight to his other leg. "They're in Jackson County, working a scene as we speak. And I'll be long gone by the time they discover your body."

Pure terror flew through Tina. He'd said *body*. He had definitely come to kill her.

She flinched when he reached up to touch her face, prompting a manic-sounding laugh from him.

"Are you afraid of me, Tina?"

When she only stared straight ahead, he gripped her by the chin, forcing her gaze to his.

"You can relax. I have plans for you before I kill you."

More terror slid through her. What was he going to do to her?

Releasing her face, he pulled his T-shirt over his head and tossed it somewhere behind him.

He then straddled her lap, his hands sinking into her hair. "Kiss me, Tina."

She instinctively clamped her mouth shut.

Levi leaned in and covered her mouth with his.

Tina was unable to prevent the gag that rushed up on her.

He pulled back slightly, dragged his lips across her injured jaw and down to her neck. Using his nose, he nudged the strap of her tank top aside and sank his teeth into her shoulder.

Tina screamed from the sheer agony of the bite, but there was no breaking his hold. Not with her arms secured firmly behind that chair.

Levi lifted his head. "Hurts, doesn't it?"

He then brought his bandaged arm up. "Do you see what you did, Tina? I went through the windshield. Do you know what it's like to be thrown through glass at a high rate of speed?"

Tina couldn't breathe. Her face throbbed where he'd slammed his fist against it, and the bite mark on her shoulder felt like he'd branded her with fire.

"I asked you a question!" he yelled, forcing a cry of terror from her.

"N-no. I don't."

He lowered his face to her other shoulder. "I didn't think so."

Another bite, harder this time.

Tina tried to buck him off, to no avail. The hoarse scream ripping from her throat only seemed to spur him on.

"I'm sorry!" she cried, her entire body shaking in pain. "Ah, God, I'm sorry!"

He bit her again.

And on it went with him biting her and then kissing the marks he left behind.

Tina had never felt so much agony in her life. Not even the injury in her thigh hurt on this level.

And Levi knew that. He knew exactly what to do to cause the most suffering. He enjoyed inflicting it, got off on her tormented cries.

In that moment, something shifted inside Tina. No matter how much pain he forced upon her, she wouldn't give him the satisfaction of hearing her cry.

He bit her again on the side of her upper arm.

Tina locked her teeth together, forcing the agony of the bite to the back of her mind.

Levi must have sensed her intentions. He pulled back enough to look down into her face. "Trying to play tough?"

Before she could process his intent, he yanked her tank top down, pinched the tender skin of her breast between his thumb and forefinger, and twisted.

The sound that came from Tina resembled that of a wounded animal. An unholy, inhuman sound that ricocheted off the walls of her small home.

"That's better," Levi praised, laughter in his voice.

He pinched the other breast, twisting it to the point where Tina nearly passed out from the excruciating torment.

Her shoulders curved forward in an effort to dislodge his hold. "Stoooop!"

"Okay." He hopped from her lap.

What horrid thing would Levi do to her next? Tina couldn't bear the thought...

Her head fell forward, her body trembling in agony.

Chapter Thirty-Eight

Mike sat next to Sheriff Mulligan in Desiree's office, going over the fax they'd received from the FBI.

He glanced over at the sheriff. "It says here that the victim was fully dressed, still wearing her seatbelt."

"Yeah," the sheriff answered, "I saw that."

Desiree waved a hand toward the paper Mike held. "What are you thinking?"

"It may be nothing." Mike shrugged for emphasis. "But the hitcher normally demeans his victims. Makes them undress, rapes them."

Mike thought about everything that Tina had witnessed and endured at the hands of Levi Ransom. Things that he would never be able to take from her. No matter how badly he wanted to.

"And it doesn't appear that this last vic was sexually assaulted," the sheriff pointed out.

Desiree blew out a breath and leaned back in her chair. "We don't know that for sure. We have no idea how much time he spent with her before he killed her."

Mulligan nodded. "True, but why redress the body when he didn't bother with the others?"

"He's angry," Mike muttered softly. "He knows he's as good as caught. This last murder wasn't about taking satisfaction in tormenting his victim. He's losing control."

"But why?" Desiree asked, looking from one man to the other. "What set him off?"

Mike met her gaze. "Because his prize got away."

Mulligan ran a hand through his hair. "Tina."

"Exactly," Mike confirmed, turning to face the sheriff. "She not only got away, but she injured him. In his mind, she bested him."

Suddenly sick to his stomach, Mike pushed to his feet. "I'm getting out of here. Once you hear anything about the latest vic, will you give me a call?"

The sheriff stood also. "Will do. Please let Tina know we're thinking of her and to take all the time she needs. Her job will be right here when she's ready to return."

If she returns, Mike thought to himself. "I'll let her know, sir."

Mike left the station by way of the backdoor. He trudged across the parking area, unlocked his car, and slid behind the wheel.

The interior of his vehicle felt hot enough to fry an egg. He started the engine and switched on the blessed air conditioning.

Backing out, he turned the car toward town. He would buy Tina some flowers, grab some food for the motorhome, and take her out of town. Someplace far from Florida... Far from the nightmare of the hitcher.

His cell phone rang as he pulled out into traffic. Mike snatched it up and brought it to his ear. "Parker."

"Mr. Parker? This is Martha Shoemaker. I'm the general manager for one of your car lots." She rattled off the name of the dealership. "I was wondering if you would have some time this week to sit down and go over some of the inventory items with me. I also need to discuss a few of the employees with you, as well as which vehicles go on sale and —"

"I'm sorry to interrupt you, Martha, but I have a bit of an emergency going on at the moment. I'll be out of town for a week or so. Is there any way you can hold off on this meeting until I return?"

She made an apologetic sound. "Of course, sir. Take your time. There's no emergency. Just give me a call when you're ready, and I'll schedule something with you then."

"Sure thing, Miss. Shoemaker. Text me a good number where you can be reached, and I'll call you once I get back in town."

"You got it. Enjoy your trip, sir." She ended the call.

Mike knew he had responsibilities with the dealerships he now owned. But Tina came first. And what she needed at the moment was time away from the nightmare that had become her life since her encounter with the hitcher.

She needed relaxation, a change in scenery. She needed to laugh and try new foods. To forget what she'd been through, even if for just a short time.

Mike pulled into the parking lot of the local florist, Tina strong on his mind. He would grab her two dozen roses, some chocolates, and a nice card.

That should brighten her day.

Chapter Thirty-Nine

Tina watched Levi through swollen eyes and a haze of agonizing pain. Over the past hour, he had struck her, bit her, and kicked her more times than she could remember.

She'd blacked out several times from being struck in the face, but he always managed to force her out of the darkness.

A moan rumbled in her throat.

"What's that?" he asked in a breathy voice. "You want to play? Well, sure we can. What would you like to play?"

When she didn't answer, not that she could, he pretended to consider his options.

"Ah, I got it! This is the best game of all. You're going to thoroughly enjoy it."

He half leaned across her and plucked up the revolver lying on the table.

"Ever played Russian roulette?" He flipped open the revolver, emptied the bullets onto the table, and plucked up one, which he quickly replaced.

Tina stared in horror as he spun the cylinder before snapping it into place.

He pulled the hammer back. "Open your mouth."

"Oh God," she half groaned, half croaked, her pain suddenly forgotten.

She would die shortly. He would torment her with the terror of pulling that trigger, again and again, until that bullet reached its destination.

"God? Why call on God? I'm the one holding your life in my hands. Beg me to let you live."

She knew he wouldn't let her live, whether she begged him or not.

"No?" He forced the barrel inside her mouth and pulled the trigger.

Tina burst into tears, uncontrollable sobs escaping from her as she choked on the barrel of that revolver.

"Shhhhh," he shushed her, running his free hand through her hair. "All you have to do is ask me nicely, and I'll let you live. It's as simple as that."

Liar, she wanted to scream, seeing the evidence of his intent in his psychotic-looking eyes.

"I'm still seeing rebellion in you, my love. If you don't want to play nice, then I can do this all day. I have nothing but time."

He pulled the trigger once more.

The click sounded like an explosion in Tina's desperate mind.

She couldn't stop the panicked cry that flew from her throat.

Levi abruptly removed the gun from her mouth. He spun the cylinder again and again, flipping it open and then closed.

"Kill me!" Tina screamed, unable to stand the sounds that revolver made a second longer. She knew that he was purposely dragging out her death to torment her. "Just kill me and get it over with!"

He laughed in her face. "Such brave talk from the one about to shake the legs off that chair."

"Screw you!"

"Now that's the best idea you've had yet." He pulled a knife from the back pocket of his jeans and stepped around behind her.

She could feel him cutting through the tape until her wrists were free.

He then dropped to his haunches in front of her and cut her ankles loose.

Grabbing her by the hair, he yanked her to her feet.

Tina went wild, fighting him with everything she had in her. Which wasn't much in her condition, but fear fed her panic, and panic lent her strength.

She swung out, her elbow connecting with his throat.

He released her briefly but had her hair back inside his fist before she could take a step forward. "You're going to pay for that."

Levi dragged her toward her bedroom, the pain in her scalp almost unbearable.

He shoved her forward, tossing her onto her bed and following her down.

The gun was back in her face. "Put your arms above your head."

Tina had no intention of obeying him. She was dead no matter what she did. If he were going to rape her, he would have to rape her corpse.

She spit in his face.

Rage swirled through his eyes, mixed with an insanity the likes of which she could never have imagined.

He dropped the gun next to him on the bed, grabbed her wrists, and yanked her arms above her head, where he gripped them tightly in one of his large hands.

Tina fought to free herself, to no avail. She was no match for his strength. Especially the superhuman strength of a man insane.

With his free hand, he tore her shorts from her body.

Chapter Forty

Mike dialed Tina's cell phone to let her know he was on his way. He'd forgone the grocery store, deciding instead to take her out for sushi and wine. Two of her favorite things on the planet.

It rang several times before going to voicemail.

Odd, he thought, trying her again only to get the same result.

Attempting to keep his gaze on the road, he scrolled through his cell until he located the number for Sam, the deputy assigned to keep an eye on Tina.

No answer.

Mike dropped his cell phone on the console and punched the gas. Something was wrong.

His stomach was a ball of nerves by the time he reached Tina's place.

A candy-apple-red hatchback was parked along the edge of the road several yards from Tina's drive.

Mike pulled up behind the vehicle and jumped out. He checked the inside of the car to find it empty.

His heart pounding erratically, he pulled his weapon, cocked it, and jogged through the trees to the unmarked car in the drive.

Sam lay over in the seat in a pool of blood, his eyes open and set. He'd been dead for a while.

Horror and disbelief slammed into Mike. *Tina!*

Hurrying along the edge of the drive, Mike bypassed the front door and darted around back.

No sounds could be heard from inside. He couldn't be too late. He refused to believe it.

With unsteady hands, he gripped the handle of the sliding doors, relieved to find it unlocked.

As quietly as possible, he eased the door open enough to slip inside, his eyes and ears alert.

Locking both hands on the butt of his gun, he swung it in both directions, only to find the kitchen and dining room empty.

And then, a faint sound came from Tina's bedroom, followed by another.

Mike stalked his way down the hallway, his weapon at the ready, until he arrived at Tina's bedroom.

What he saw there sent him over the edge.

Tina lay on her back on her bed, her face bloodied and bruised beyond recognition. Her tank top was down around her waist, and her shorts had been removed.

Levi Ransom straddled her hips, holding her arms above her head in one of his hands, his other on the zipper of his jeans.

Mike couldn't think beyond the image of Tina's distorted, terrified face.

A primitive roar exploded from his chest. He took aim at Levi's forehead and pulled the trigger.

Levi's body flew backward and dropped heavily to the floor.

Mike rushed into the room and scrambled onto the bed. "Tina!"

A horrific scream resounded throughout the room, a haunting sound that Mike would likely never forget.

Tina's eyes were unfocused, her mouth open to release another hoarse, bloodcurdling scream.

She jerked upward, her arms swinging wildly, all the while that inhuman sound ripping from her throat.

Mike dove on her, wrapping his arms tightly around her. "Tina, baby, it's me, Mike! I'm here. You're okay. Shhhhh. It's okay now."

A shudder passed through her body and then another. "M-Mike?"

"Shhhhh, I'm here. I've got you."

She suddenly went limp in his arms.

Mike pulled back enough to see her battered face. A tear rolled off his chin to mingle with the blood on her cheek.

"I'm so sorry, baby. God, I'm so sorry."

He pulled her tightly against his chest, rocking her back and forth in his arms. He hadn't been there for her. She had faced that demon once again by herself.

Long moments passed with Mike refusing to let Tina go. But he knew he had to. He needed to take her to the hospital and notify the sheriff's office of the two deaths.

Careful of the precious burden in his arms, Mike lifted Tina higher against his chest and got to his feet.

He carried her out of the house and to his vehicle waiting on the side of the road.

Tears still dripped off his chin as uncontrollable emotions held him in their grip.

Rage, disbelief, sorrow, love, and pain all warred within him, until he had to fight for every breath he took.

Opening the passenger side door, he gently placed Tina on the seat, started the engine, and snatched up his cell phone.

The air conditioner had been left on and now blew ice-cold air throughout the car's interior.

Quietly closing Tina's door, Mike dialed 911, as was protocol. He gave the dispatcher his name and Tina's address. Then, he reported the shooting, the death of the deputy, and the home invasion.

Ending the call against the dispatcher's orders, Mike notified Sheriff Mulligan of what had happened and then drove like the wind to the closest hospital.

He pulled up beneath the pavilion in front of the emergency room and jumped out, adrenaline riding his every step.

"Do you need some help?" a nurse called out as Mike opened the passenger side door of his car.

He leaned in and carefully extracted Tina's limp form from the seat. "She's hurt pretty bad."

"Follow me!" The nurse ran ahead, clearing a path through the swaths of sick and injured, coming to a stop next to a sheet-covered gurney.

As gently as he could manage, Mike placed Tina's body on top of that gurney while answering the dozens of questions being asked of him—Tina's name, birthdate, and cause of her injuries.

An IV was started immediately. "Do you know if she's allergic to any medications?" the nurse asked.

"I— No, I don't think so."

"I'm not," Tina whispered, drawing Mike's attention to her face.

"You're not what?" The sound of her voice, no matter how weak, was music to his ears.

"Not...allergic."

Mike quickly took hold of her hand, bent, and brought it to his lips.

"Don't cry," she wheezed so softly he almost didn't hear her.

He hadn't even realized he still cried.

Chapter Forty-One

Through swollen eyes, Tina stared at Mike's sleeping form slouched in a chair next to her hospital bed. He'd stayed in the room with her last night.

Bits and pieces of the day before played through her mind, tormenting her with their memories.

Levi had inserted the barrel of his revolver into her mouth and forced her to play Russian roulette.

Tina couldn't describe the feeling of hearing that click, knowing that she'd survived, only to have to do it again.

She swallowed, her throat raw and burning from the screams of Levi's torture sessions. She had thought for sure that she would die. Yet there she lay, fortunate enough to live another day with Mike Parker.

Mike had saved her. He'd arrived just in time to prevent her from being sexually assaulted, by putting a bullet between Levi's eyes.

"I love you, Mike Parker," she softly whispered, her gaze touching on every inch of the man she would spend the rest of her life with.

His eyes fluttered open, and the corner of his mouth lifted. "If you want me under that sheet with you, that's the quickest way to make it happen."

Tina would have laughed if it didn't hurt to do so. "Well, come here, then…"

Epilogue

Two years later

Tina swam to the deep end of the pool and tossed the rubber bone she held to the shallow end. "Go get it!"

A very healthy, happy Buddy bounded in after it, with the rest of the crew right on his heels.

Four other dogs of various sizes and shapes dove in behind him, all excited to reach the bone first.

"Why don't we adopt one more," Mike teased while flipping the steaks on the grill. "Make it an even six."

Tina laughed, meeting his gaze. "Don't tempt me."

Bobbi eased down the ladder of the pool next to Tina, her fifteen-month-old son in her arms. "You don't need more dogs, crazy woman."

"And you don't need any more kids," Tina teased, glancing beneath the water at Bobbi's swollen belly.

Bobbi laughed. "Touché."

Tina returned her friend's smile and then flicked her gaze over to Joey, helping Mike with the grill.

Joey had been sober since the day he'd nearly lost his wife and unborn son. The couple had continuously grown closer, leaving Bobbi a happy, glowing wife and mother.

Mike and Tina had settled into their new lives as well. The house had plenty of room for all the pets, as did the yard.

And going on road trips with the animals wasn't an issue, since they'd traded in their motorhome and purchased a much larger one with three slide-outs.

Mike had retired from the sheriff's office less than a week after he'd shot and killed Levi Ransom.

After meeting with Martha Shoemaker, Mike had jumped into the car business like he did everything else... Feet first.

It didn't take him long to figure everything out, which didn't surprise Tina in the least. He had more common sense than any man she'd ever known. And was better looking, she silently admitted, listening to his laughter.

Tina, on the other hand, still worked part time for animal control but only as a floater. If someone called out sick or went on vacation, she would fill the position until their return. Otherwise, she and Mike spent their days in marital bliss.

Tina tried not to think about that horrific weekend from her past when she'd nearly died, that terrible day when Roslynn lost her life.

But she wasn't always successful.

Sometimes, late at night when Mike softly snored next to her, when the moon rose high overhead and the bullfrogs croaked in the distance, Tina would lie awake at night and remember every sickening detail of Roslynn's terrified screams and the psychotic blue eyes of...the hitcher.

If you enjoyed *The Hitcher*, read below for a sneak peek into the pages of *Silence of the Whippoorwill: A Bone-Chilling Psychological Thriller* and *I Am Elle: A Psychological Thriller*.

Chapter One

"I'm having a hard time going to sleep," Breezy Anderson admitted, staring up at the slow-moving ceiling fan in the vacation rental she shared with her longtime friend, Nancy Blaylock.

Nancy blew out a breath and rolled to her side to face Breezy. "I gave you some over-the-counter sleep aid. Didn't you take it?"

Breezy shot her friend a sideways look. "The gang will be ready to leave before daylight. If I took the sleep aid, I'd never be able to get up by four a.m."

"And if you *don't* take it, you'll not be up in time to depart. Neither will I, since I can hear you over there flopping around."

Breezy laughed. "Touché."

"Is something bothering you, maybe something you'd like to talk about?"

Breezy snatched up the sleeping pills and washed them down with a glass of water that sat on the nightstand. "I've just got a lot going on in my life right now. Nothing I can't handle though."

"Is it your parents?" Nancy persisted, propping her head up on the palm of her hand.

Thinking of her parents' inevitable divorce sent a sinking feeling into the pit of Breezy's stomach. The two of them had been married for twenty-five-years, raising Breezy to the best of their ability. It broke her heart to imagine them going their separate ways. "Maybe."

"People divorce, Breezy. It happens every day. It's a sad reality of life, but that doesn't mean it has to be the end of the world. Your parents are on friendly terms. Take solace in that."

Breezy knew her friend spoke the truth. Nancy had been a psychology major at Florida

State University for the past four years. She understood the workings of the mind as well as the heart.

Shifting her gaze to Nancy, Breezy sent her a reassuring smile. "I'm going to miss you, ya know."

Nancy, Breezy, and the other members of their small group had been friends since elementary school. Some of them had gone off to college, while others took jobs locally in the Panhandle of Florida.

But no matter where life took the crew of lifelong friends, they always managed to stay in touch and meet up once a year to do something they'd never done before. This year's trip consisted of hiking in the mountains of Arkansas.

A sadness entered Nancy's eyes. "I'll miss you too, Breezy. This will be my last trip with you guys for a while."

"Are you really moving to California?" Though Breezy was proud of Nancy for following her dreams to practice psychology in Santa Barbara, she hated more than anything to see her go.

Nancy sighed in the dark. "Think of it this way, it'll give you some place exciting to visit me in the future."

Breezy yawned, the effects of the sleep aid beginning to kick in. "This is true. If we survive this hike up the mountains, that is."

"You mean, if *I* survive," Nancy pointed out with a chuckle. "I'm the pansy in our group. You're tough as nails, Deputy Anderson. You're likely to scale that mountain and pop up somewhere in Missouri before we finish our first mile."

"Don't sell yourself short, Dr. Blaylock," Breezy shot back with emphasis on the word *doctor*. "I've seen you manage a yoga position that I'd never be able to twist my body into. You'd probably beat all of us to Missouri by way of the treetops."

The two of them shared a laugh for long moments before Breezy sobered. She rolled to her side to face the wall, hoping Nancy wouldn't pick up on her despondency.

The divorce of Breezy's parents wasn't the only heartache on the young deputy's mind. Lucas, her significant other for the past two years, had been unfaithful. And if there was one thing Breezy detested more than anything, it was a cheat.

Breezy had suggested Lucas pack his bags and be gone by the time she returned from her trip, else she would burn them. And she'd meant it.

Chapter Two

Breezy watched the members of her group strap on their gear and prepare for their three-day trek through the mountains.

The joking and simple camaraderie did her heart good. She brushed off the feelings of betrayal she'd had for the past few days and moved forward to join them.

Janine Foreman shot Breezy a wink while reaching to take hold of Dale Hastings' hand. Dale and Janine had been dating since junior high. And though the two were obviously in love, they tended to fight like two tomcats in the same vicinity of a female cat in heat.

"Are you ready for this, Deputy?" Janine's blue eyes twinkled with humor. Her blonde hair had been pulled back into a severe ponytail, enhancing her perfect cheekbones.

Dale tugged Janine close to his side, his humorous gaze flashing to Breezy. "Don't pay her any mind. She wouldn't be out here without me, for fear she might break a nail."

Janine playfully smacked Dale on the arm. "Whatever, you chest-slapping ape. You weren't complaining about my nails last night when we were—"

"Okay then," Dane Watson interrupted, cutting off the rest of Janine's words. "No one wants to hear about your romp in the hay with ole Dale, here. That's not a visual I want while hiking through the thicket."

Dane was the thinker in the group. With her auburn hair and green eyes, she'd been attending the University of Florida for the past four years while majoring in business. Aside from being smart, she happened to be the most levelheaded person Breezy knew.

Teri Roberts stepped forward, her platinum-blonde hair piled up on top of her head in a loose knot. "Where is our guide?" She glanced at her waterproof watch. "He's late."

"Easy there, princess," Steven Billings teased, the porch light from a nearby cabin reflecting off his freshly shaved head. "There's no need to be in a hurry. We're about to embark on a three-day journey up the mountain, with no amenities to speak of. So, if you need to pee, now's the time to do it."

"Pee," Teri gasped, her mouth falling open in feigned shock. "Are you sure you're not from around here?"

He flashed a smile, showing off his perfect white teeth. "Do I look like I'm from these parts?"

"What's that s'pose to mean," a voice drawled from the shadows.

Breezy jerked her gaze in the direction of the voice in time to see an older, slightly overweight man step into the light. A deep scar ran from his right eyebrow and down his cheek. He had pockmarks on his face, and his thinning brown combover lay across his forehead in a tangled, greasy mess. Her gaze lowered still, to a large buck knife strapped to the side of the man's stained-up jeans.

"Name's Tom. And I'll be taking you down the river to your destination." He jerked his chin in the direction of a trail that led to the water's edge. "Boat's down yonder."

Everyone began to move toward the trail Tom had indicated. Everyone except Breezy. She stood rooted to the spot, her focus on their guide.

Something about the guy, other than his obviously poor hygiene, raised the fine hairs on the back of her neck.

"Is there a problem?" he asked, staring back at her through narrowed eyes.

Breezy stood her ground. "What did you say your last name was again?"

"I didn't."

"Well?" Breezy prompted when he didn't elaborate.

"Name's Tom Berry. And it's gettin' late, so we better go if we're goin'."

Breezy's intuition screamed for her not to trust Tom. Something about the man felt off.

"Look, lady. I've got other tours I'm s'pose to lead before sunup, and we have prayer meetin' tonight, which means the church needs cleanin'."

Relaxing her shoulders at the mention of church, Breezy gave a curt nod and struck out to catch up with her group.

She could feel the unwashed guide's gaze boring into her back as she made her way down the trail to the boat.

Everyone was situated in the craft, impatience fairly oozing from their pores.

Nancy raised her eyebrows, shooting Breezy a questioning look.

Not wanting to be the cause of undue worry, Breezy sent her friend a wink and boarded the boat.

Tom climbed in last, cranked the motor, and the boat took off with a jolt.

The ride down the river took Breezy's breath away. Massive rock formations lined her left, giving the appearance of multiple calico blankets.

Trees on the right side of the bank could be seen for miles, rising up from the earth in a canopy of nature that couldn't have been painted more perfectly. The sun reflected off the crystal-clear water, giving an illusion of diamonds floating on the surface. It had to be the most beautiful sight Breezy had ever beheld.

The boat came to a stop about twenty minutes later. Tom jumped out first, dragged the vessel onto the bank, and waited for the group to depart. "I'll be back to get y'all at noon in three days at this same spot. If you ain't here, you'll have to walk back or wait for the next guide to come along. *If* one comes along."

What an odd thing to say, Breezy thought, hoisting her backpack straps onto her shoulders and hiking up the hill. *An odd thing indeed…*

Chapter Three

Breezy exited the tree line after doing her business in the woods. A fire burned in the center of their camp, illuminating the faces of their small group.

Nancy sat on a log next to Steven, laughing at something he'd whispered for only her to hear.

Janine, of course, was perched on Dale's lap, her face buried against his neck.

Dane and Teri were passing a whiskey bottle between them while staring into the flames of the fire.

The call of a whippoorwill suddenly echoed in the distance, a mournful sound that resonated within Breezy's soul.

She'd only heard the elusive bird's call maybe a dozen times in her life. Of course, with Florida being an overly crowded tourist state, it was no wonder the birds had moved on to other territories. Condos now stood on nearly every square inch of the Panhandle, forcing a lot of wildlife to migrate north. Other than fish and mosquitos. There were plenty of fish and mosquitos.

Her father had also told her that the number of whippoorwills appeared to have decreased over much of the east in recent decades. Reasons for the decline, he wasn't sure, but he stated that it could reflect a general reduction in the numbers of large moths and beetles, which were the whippoorwill's main diet.

Entering the campsite, Breezy eased down onto a log close to Teri. "Do you hear that whippoorwill song? It's the most soulful sound I've ever heard. Reminds me of my grandfather. Of late nights, chasing lightning bugs. The smell of Granny's apple pie. The taste of her buttermilk biscuits, fresh from the oven. I figured the birds would have migrated south by now, with winter just around the corner."

Steven accepted the bottle of whiskey being passed in his direction. He took a long pull and then met Breezy's gaze across the campfire. "The migration will begin next month. It's not cold enough yet."

"Makes sense," Breezy agreed, allowing the bird's song to wash through her once more.

Steven spoke again. "You do know what that song means, don't you?"

Breezy shrugged. "According to my dad, the male eastern whippoorwill makes that sound at night in order to establish their territory or attract a mate."

Steven's eyes glittered in the firelight. "That's true to a point."

"Meaning?" Breezy pressed, stretching her legs out in front of her and crossing her booted feet at the ankles.

Steven took another drink of the whiskey, wiped his mouth with the back of his hand, and sent Breezy a penetrating stare. "According to mythology, a whippoorwill singing near a house is an omen of death or at least of bad luck."

The bird's song came again, sending chills peppering along Breezy's skin.

"*If* you believe in that sort of thing," Steven continued before guzzling more of the whiskey.

Breezy gazed around the campsite, noticing everyone's attention riveted on Steven. She cleared her throat. "Of course I don't believe in it. It's a load of bull, probably told around similar campfires by similar idiots."

Steven chuckled, handing the bottle to Nancy. "Are you calling me an idiot?"

"I am," Breezy shot back, her lips twitching.

Dale suddenly stood, taking Janine with him. He snatched up a blanket and disappeared into the shadows, calling over his shoulder as he went, "Keep the fire stoked while we're gone."

"Freaks," Breezy teased, staring at their retreating backs. She inwardly sighed. She and Lucas used to be spontaneous like that. There was a time when he couldn't have kept his hands off her either. But that was before he'd ended up in the arms of a sleazy blonde dispatcher who'd frequented half the beds of the county's entire fire department.

"A penny for your thoughts," Dane murmured softly, leaning around Teri in order to see Breezy's face.

Realizing her pain probably showed, Breezy stood and retrieved the whiskey bottle from Nancy. She took a swig to buy herself some time and then returned to her previous position on the log. "I was just thinking about work."

Dane clucked her tongue. "You should have left work back in Florida. This is our last year of vacationing together for God knows how long. Nancy and I are leaving after graduation, and Dale and Janine are getting married. At the rate you and Lucas are going, I wouldn't doubt that you'll be hitched shortly thereafter. Life is changing for us all, but for the better. So, lighten up, honey."

Breezy blanked her expression. She would wait until they returned home to inform the group about her split with Lucas. "You're right, of course. This is our last trip together for a while, and I intend to make it the best one yet."

No one spoke for long moments, and then Teri pushed to her feet. She stretched, locking her wrists and pushing her arms above her head. A jaw-popping yawn ensued. "I'm going to get some sleep." She glanced at her watch. "I'll see you all in the morning."

"Who's catching breakfast?" Dane moved to stand as well.

"Not it," Breezy blurted with a chuckle.

Everyone else followed suit, with Steven being the last to speak.

Breezy grinned at him over the top of the fire. "Looks like you'll be handling the fishing, bright and early, my man. Unless you'd rather dine on granola bars and jerky."

"Y'all suck," he muttered, rising and stumbling toward his tent.

Everyone dispersed, leaving Breezy to sit alone by the fire. She could hear Janine and Dale giggling in the distance, a sound that brought more pain.

It wasn't that Breezy begrudged them their happiness. On the contrary, she loved the pair like family. But seeing them so in love brought home the fact that no man had ever been faithful to her the way Dale had always been faithful to Janine. And…it hurt.

Breezy sighed into the night, her gaze locked on the flames of the fire. *Goodbye, Lucas.*

The whippoorwill's song once again shattered the night, reminding her of Steven's words. *"According to mythology, a whippoorwill singing near a house is an omen of death."*

Good thing I don't believe in old wives' tales, Breezy thought, shaking her head at the ridiculousness of Steven's chilling words. She closed her eyes, allowing the consistent call of that bird to lull her into a state of melancholy.

And then a strange sensation washed over her, a feeling Breezy had come to recognize from her years as an officer of the law. She was being watched.

The whippoorwill called again…

Chapter Four

Breezy remained completely still for long moments, listening, expanding her senses to her surroundings.

She opened her eyes, her gaze scanning the darkness beyond the camp. But nothing moved.

Slowly getting to her feet, she glanced toward her tent, the tent where her backpack lay. The backpack that contained her knife.

I'm being silly, she told herself, forcing her body to relax while making her way to her tent. *Steven is to blame for my paranoia, with his old wives' whippoorwill tale. I should yank him up and send him out to check the woods.*

But the closer Breezy got to her tent, the stronger the eerie sensation grew.

She pushed the flap aside and entered, fishing her knife out of her backpack before returning to the edge of the fire.

With knife in hand, Breezy swallowed her apprehension and headed into the tree line.

Her eyes quickly adjusted to the darkness. She held that blade in a tight grip, forcing her feet to take her deeper into the forest.

A twig snapped somewhere to her left, sounding like a gunshot in the otherwise quiet night.

Breezy stilled, her heart hammering loud enough to drown out her senses.

The sound came again, closer this time.

Easing her back against a tree, she homed in on her surroundings. Whoever it was out there, they were definitely close.

Another twig snapped, not three feet behind her. With her heart in her throat, Breezy held that knife handle in a white-knuckled grip, locked her teeth together, and pushed away from the tree.

A racoon suddenly scrambled away, startling Breezy as much as she'd startled it. She blew out a half sigh, half shaky laugh and lowered her knife. "You better run, you little turd."

A figure abruptly sprang from the shadows faster than Breezy's eyes could track. She jerked her knife up and swung wide.

"Whoa," Dale burst out, jumping back a few feet, his hands instantly up. "Easy there, Sarah Conner. It's just us."

It took a second for Breezy to grasp that Dale and Janine stood in front of her and another to realize she'd nearly stabbed one of them.

"Jesus, Dale, I could've killed you!"

Dale laughed nervously. "Sorry, but we saw you out here slinking about and thought we'd give you a little scare. What are you doing out here anyway? And with a two-foot butcher knife, no less."

Realizing she still held the blade out in front of her, Breezy lowered it. "Well, your scare tactic worked. I nearly crapped myself. And I wasn't slinking. I thought I heard something." She pushed past the duo and headed back to camp.

Dale and Janine followed.

"I'm sorry," Janine called out, quickly catching up. "Dale thought it would be funny. And honestly, so did I. I never thought it would upset you this much. And had I known you were carrying that Jason Voorhees machete—"

"It's not a machete, dimwit, it's a buck knife," Breezy instinctively snapped. But then the reality of the situation began to sink in. Her lips twitched.

She glanced over at the now big-eyed Janine, who still hurried anxiously along beside her. "I'm sorry about the dimwit comment."

Janine instantly laughed. "Well, I'm *not* sorry for the Voorhees reference. I call it like I see it. Where did you get that thing anyway?"

Breezy folded the knife and tucked it inside her boot. "Lucas bought it for me during hunting season last year."

"But you don't hunt," Janine unnecessarily pointed out. "You're one of the biggest animal activists I've ever known."

"I didn't say I used it to hunt with. I merely pointed out where it came from."

Janine continued to traipse along beside Breezy. "Fair enough. I meant to ask earlier. Where is Lucas anyway? Wasn't he supposed to come on this trip?"

The thought of her soon-to-be ex sent pain slicing through Breezy's heart. She opened her mouth to tell Janine that Lucas was likely in the arms of his current side piece but decided against it. The admission would only elicit pity. And Breezy detested pity of any kind. So she lied. "He couldn't get off work."

Janine seemed to accept the explanation without question. "That's too bad."

The trio arrived back at camp, with Dale nearly tripping over one of the logs resting next to the fire.

Breezy grinned. "Serves you right. You better take your drunk self to bed before you catch the entire camp on fire."

With a salute and a lopsided smile, Dale grabbed onto Janine's hand. "Best idea I've heard all night."

Breezy watched them go, listening to Janine's playful banter as she ducked inside the tent.

Making her way to the center of camp, Breezy put out the fire, finished off the bottle of whiskey still perched on a log, and then entered her tent.

She knelt to remove her boots but changed her mind, opting to sleep fully dressed instead.

Though winter hadn't officially arrived, she'd been told by their trip advisor that the temperature in the mountains of Arkansas dropped significantly at night. Enough so that Breezy had been sure to bring along some warm clothes.

Slipping inside her sleeping bag, she rolled to her side and attempted to block out the sounds coming from Janine and Dale's tent.

Her eyes eventually drifted shut.

A sample of I Am Elle: A Psychological Thriller

Prologue

Wexler, Alabama

Population 2415

"Elle!" Elijah Griffin shouted, the back door slamming in the distance, a testament to his mood.

He'd been drinking again.

Elenore hovered behind the chicken coop, her bare feet catching on briars in her haste to escape her father.

"Elle Griffin? So help me God, girl, I will take my belt to you if you don't bring your butt here at once!"

She didn't want to leave the safety the shadows of the chicken coop provided. But she was afraid not to.

If she remained there, and her father found her hiding from him, he would hurt her. Badly.

Tears gathered in her eyes, but she blinked them back. One thing Elijah Griffin hated worse than disobedience was tears.

Elenore wiped at her eyes with the hem of her dress and stepped from behind the coop.

The evening sun had begun its descent, casting shadows along the side of the house and hiding her father's expression from view.

But Elenore didn't need to see his face to understand what he wanted from her, what he'd been taking from her for years.

She lowered her head and slowly moved in his direction.

"Where've you been, girl?" He gripped her upper arm in a painful hold. "Get your butt in that house."

Elenore stumbled toward the steps at the back door. She swallowed back the panic that rose in her throat at the knowledge of the horror that awaited her inside.

She could feel her father tight on her heels, knew he would be on her within seconds.

But hard as she tried, Elenore could fight the tears no longer.

And the tears would make it worse...so much worse.

"Are you crying?" he slurred, his hand suddenly in her hair.

He jerked her around to face him. "What have I told you about crybabies?"

"I-I won't do it again."

He stared at her for achingly long moments, unsteady on his feet. "Get in your room."

Elenore didn't want to go into her room. She knew what would happen to her once inside.

He backhanded her across the face.

The copper taste of blood filled her mouth.

With her jaw now throbbing to the beat of her heart, Elenore staggered toward her bedroom door, Elijah following close behind.

She could hear the buckle of his belt tinkering as he released it and slid it free of his beltloops. She turned to face him.

"Take it off," he demanded, nodding to her dress.

Her fingers trembled so badly they barely functioned.

He took a step toward her. "Now!"

Elenore jumped, lifting her shaky fingers to the first button at the top of her dress.

There would be no stopping her father from what he intended to do to her. There never was.

Elenore took a slow, deep breath, lifting her gaze to a place just beyond his shoulder. She forced her eyes to relax until the wall behind him faded into the distance. Her vision grew tunneled, and her mind floated off to a place where nothing or no one could touch her. Especially not her father...

Chapter One

Ten Years Later

Elenore kept her gaze on the floor and accepted the two bags of groceries the bag boy handed her.

"Do you need some help carrying them to your car?"

She knew the bag boy spoke to her, but she pretended not to hear him. Besides, if he saw that she didn't have a car, there would be no hiding the pity that would surely come.

And Elenore hated pity, nearly as much as she despised her father's pet name for her. *Elle.* It wasn't so much the name itself as the way he said it...like a caress. She inwardly shuddered.

"No, thank you," Elenore whispered, scurrying off in the direction of the automatic doors.

The noonday sun beamed overhead, temporarily blinding her with its intensity.

She squinted against the brightness and hoisted the groceries up higher in her arms. She had a two mile walk ahead of her, and she needed to hurry if she thought to have dinner ready by the time her father arrived home.

The bags grew heavier the longer Elenore walked, until she thought for sure her arms would fall off.

A truck slowed to a stop beside her. "Need a lift?"

Elenore wanted to say yes, but of course, she didn't. Too many questions would be asked. She'd had her run-in with some of the town folk in the past, which only served to anger her father.

She shook her head and continued on.

"Suit yourself." The truck drove away.

Elenore arrived home approximately forty minutes after leaving the grocery store. Her feet ached almost as much as her arms did.

At least her father wasn't home. For that, she was grateful.

Since Elenore was no longer a minor, the state of Alabama had cut off any financial help Elijah had been receiving after his wife left him twelve years earlier.

He'd been forced to work on a more permanent basis, which afforded Elenore a daily reprieve from his presence. She loved being alone, with no one around but her animals.

Now that Elijah had a little money, he usually spent it on card games and prostitutes, which kept him busy more often than not.

Today would be a "not" day.

After putting the meager amount of groceries away, Elenore tied an apron around her waist and strode out to the chicken coop to gather the eggs.

She shooed the hens aside while attempting to dodge the piles of chicken droppings in her path. If not for the eggs and occasional meat the chickens provided, Elenore would go hungry.

Elijah left thirty dollars on the kitchen counter every Friday. Barely enough to buy the essentials, such as toilet paper and shampoo, let alone bread and canned foods.

So, Elenore had quickly learned how to budget…and shoplift anything she could fit in her pockets.

Once the eggs were gathered, she took out the chicken she'd killed the day before and started dinner.

Elenore had learned at an early age to shut down her emotions and do what had to be done. Besides, she told herself, killing a chicken was essential to her survival. *Nothing more.*

The old clapboard house she shared with her father quickly grew hot after turning on the oven. Even with the windows open, it became stifling. If not for the giant oak trees surrounding the house, she would probably be forced to cook outside.

Elenore wiped at her damp forehead with the back of her hand and switched on the television to watch the local news.

A pretty blonde anchorwoman sat behind a horseshoe-shaped desk, her red lipstick gleaming in the overhead lights. She spoke into the camera. *"Alan Brown makes the third person reported missing in the past two months. All three men are said to be from Haverty County, Alabama."*

Pictures appeared across the screen, with each man's name resting beneath.

Elenore wiped her hands on her apron and moved closer to the television.

"Hector Gonzalez," the anchorwoman continued, "*was last seen nearly eight weeks ago at his place of employment. Dennis Baker went missing approximately a week later. And now, Alan Brown has disappeared. If you have seen or have information on the whereabouts of any of these men, we urge you to contact the Haverty County Sheriff's Department immediately.*"

The sound of a vehicle pulling up out front brought Elenore's head up. Her father was home.

She quickly switched off the television and hurried back to the kitchen to check on the biscuits.

His truck door slammed, filling Elenore with dread. There would be only one reason for his early arrival home… He'd been drinking.

He stomped his way up the back steps to the kitchen and threw open the door. "Elle!"

Elenore could smell the liquor on his breath long before he leaned down and spoke mere inches from her face. "How long before supper?"

She backed up a step. "I—It's almost ready."

His eyes narrowed, his gaze slowly lowering to her chest. "Good. That means we have time for a father-daughter talk."

Elenore swallowed her fear. "T-talk? What would you like to talk about, Daddy?"

"Take it off."

Nausea was instant. "I— The biscuits will burn."

"I don't give a crap about biscuits." He took a step forward, his hand going around to her backside. He squeezed it painfully before jerking her hard against his body. "Do what I said, girl."

Elenore's insides turned cold. There would be no stopping him, no talking him out of what he was about to do. She'd been through it enough times to know what would come next. What always came next.

He released her, spinning her around and shoving her toward the small kitchen table against the opposite wall.

The sound of his belt coming off could be heard over the thundering of her heart.

"Turn around," he slurred.

She couldn't face him for fear she would vomit on him.

He stepped in close behind her, pressing his disgusting erection against her backside. "Turn. Around."

The vomit she fought so hard to hold back shot to her throat, hovering there in the form of bile.

He grabbed a handful of her hair and jerked her head back, his wet, disgusting mouth hovering next to her ear. "You look just like your whore of a mama."

"D-Daddy, p-please," she whispered, knowing without question that begging would do no good. It never did any good.

He twisted her hair tightly in his hold and forced her forward until her face pressed hard against the tabletop.

His free hand yanked up the hem of her dress, tossing it upward around her shoulders.

Her underwear came down next, and then the sound of his sliding zipper echoed throughout the room with haunting finality.

Elenore gripped the edges of the table in preparation of the pain she knew would come.

She bit down on the inside of her lip to keep from crying out, her gaze locked onto the wall in front of her.

She forced her eyes to relax, the sound of the table scraping across the floor beneath her fading to the background. Her vision grew tunneled until her mind slipped into a place that shut out the pain and humiliation of his invasion. A place he couldn't follow. No one could follow...

Chapter Two

Elenore awoke the following morning, her entire body throbbing in pain.

She rolled over in bed to find the sun had already risen.

Panic quickly gripped her. Her father would be up soon, wanting his breakfast.

She tossed the covers back, wincing as she threw her legs over the side of the bed.

The tenderness at the juncture of her thighs was matched only by the pain in her shoulder.

Glancing down, she took in the bruising on her upper arm, the same arm her father had held behind her back as he… She shut down her thoughts, her mind unwilling to recall what had happened to her in that kitchen.

A knock sounded on her door.

Elenore righted her tattered nightgown and surged to her feet.

Her arms instinctively crossed over her chest in anticipation of Elijah's entry.

Odd that he knocked, she thought with more than a little fear, watching intently as the doorknob turned and Elijah stepped into the room.

He stood there, staring at the floor for long moments, and then he extended a cup in her direction. "Thought you might want some orange juice."

Confusion began to mingle with her fear as it always did. The man standing before her now was not the same man who had hurt her yesterday afternoon when he got home.

He took an awkward step forward, still holding that cup in his hand. "Go on, take it."

Elenore hesitantly moved toward him and accepted the cup of juice he held. He'd offered her his juice — a juice she wasn't normally allowed to touch.

He cleared his throat. "Look, Elle. I...um... I'm sorry about yesterday. You know how I get when I've been drinking. I would never hurt you for anything in the world."

More confusion settled in.

"I love you, Elle. I don't know what I would do if you left me like your mama did. I'll stop the drinking this time. I swear it."

Elenore's heart shifted. Her father loved her. That's all she'd ever wanted from him — his love and acceptance.

Part of her loved him in return. But a part, way down deep in her soul, hated the very ground he walked on.

Tears began to gather in her eyes. Maybe he meant it this time? Maybe he realized the monster he became when drinking, and he would finally quit?

She couldn't answer him, so great was the ache in her chest. She ached to be loved, ached to run away and never look back. But mostly, she ached for revenge.

How could she simply forgive him for the pain and humiliation she'd consistently endured at his hands? Hands that should show love and compassion. The very hands he held out to her now.

Elenore took deep, calming breaths, a coping mechanism she'd learned at an early age. She forced her mind to shut out the incomprehensible memories of the day before, set her juice on the nightstand, and moved on wooden legs into her father's outstretched arms.

He gently rocked her, murmuring soothing words above her head that made little sense. "You forgive your ole man?"

She nodded, more out of habit than consent.

"Good girl." He released her and took a step back. "Don't worry about making breakfast for me. I'm going fishing with Dale Mitchell this morning. I'll just grab something on the way."

Elenore stood rooted to the spot long after her father left the room.

Her emotions were all over the place. How could a man who was supposed to love her do the things he did to her? Was it her fault?

She'd come to the conclusion over the years that she was somehow to blame for her mother leaving. And that Mary Griffin's sudden departure was the sole reason her father drank like he did.

Elenore waited until she heard Elijah's truck leave the yard before she stumbled to the bathroom and vomited.

She retched so long and hard her stomach muscles screamed in protest. Yet no matter how much she heaved, she couldn't rid herself of his smell on her.

Staggering to her feet, she turned on the shower, stripped out of her well-worn gown, and stepped under the spray.

She would scrub herself until she bled, if that's what it took to feel clean. But Elenore would never feel clean again. Never.

After her shower, she took down a green dress that had seen better days. But the sleeves were short and the material thin. Which seemed practical given the sweltering heat that was sure to arrive.

She would give anything for a pair of jeans, or pants of any kind, for that matter. But Elijah refused to let her have them. He claimed they were of the devil and reserved for men and… whores.

Slipping on the dress, she moved to stand in front of her mirror. She pulled her long blonde hair back into a ponytail and stared at her reflection. She really did resemble her mother.

Resentment boiled up inside her, the longer she stood there, looking at herself. *That is what Daddy sees when he looks at me,* she thought with more than a little disgust. *Mother.*

An image of Mary Griffin's crying face suddenly flashed through Elenore's mind. *"Elijah, don't!"*

A whimper escaped Elenore. She staggered back a few steps, her hand flying to her mouth.

The memory of Mary trying desperately to protect her daughter didn't add up with the tales Elenore had been told all her life. Even though the stories came from Elijah, Elenore had no reason not to believe him. Why else would her mother have left her behind?

According to Elijah, Mary had run off with a friend of his when Elenore was eight years old.

She'd never returned or attempted to contact her daughter in the last twelve years.

Elenore hated herself in that moment more than she'd ever hated herself before. Something was wrong with her, something bad enough that her own mother hadn't wanted her. And though her father had never walked away from her, he blamed her for her mother leaving. Elenore could see it in his eyes. Especially when he drank.

Titles by Ditter Kellen

Elle Series

I am Elle -A Psychological Thriller

Blurb:

An abused girl's desperate fight for survival and the silent killer determined to destroy her.

Born on a small farm in Alabama, Elenore Griffin spends her days in a Hell of her father's making.

The system has failed her, leaving her trapped in a world of unimaginable torture and pain.

Sold to the highest bidder, Elenore finds her nightmares have only just begun. And those responsible for her abuse begin disappearing around her without a trace, while the local authorities seem to be at the center of it all.

Step inside the world of a young girl who suffered the most heinous acts imaginable. And survived.

This is her life. This is her story...

Elle Returns– Book 2

Elle Unleashed – Book 3

Elle Freed – Book 4

The Boy in the Window

A Suspense Thriller

Blurb:

What happened to Terry Dayton?

The small community of Sparkleberry Florida is strangely tight-lipped about the disappearance of a little boy in their neighborhood. Are they covering up a thirteen-year-old murder? Jessica Nobles finds out the hard way when she moves in next door and begins unraveling the truth about 221 Meadowbrook Circle...

Jessica and Owen Nobles are heartbroken over the loss of their son, Jacob. Jessica has taken his death especially hard, spending the past three years sedated and under the care of a psychiatrist. Desperate to save his wife, Owen moves the couple to Florida, hoping a change in scenery will remind her how to live again.

When Jessica begins to see a small boy in the upstairs window of the abandoned home next door, she goes to investigate, only to find the house empty. Afraid that she may be seeing things, Jess does an internet search on the home's address. What she finds is an image of the boy from the window — a boy that's been missing more than thirteen years.

Reluctant to tell her husband, Jessica sets out to find what information she can on the child's disappearance. Yet, someone is going to great lengths to stop her.

To make matters worse, bodies begin dropping around her like flies. And she's the prime suspect in the killings. If Jessica doesn't back off now, she risks losing more than just her mind…she could very well lose her life.

The Girl Named Mud

A Gripping Suspense Novel

Blurb:

A heartbreaking story of a young girl's fight for survival in a world full of betrayal, hate, and murder...

All her life, twelve-year-old Mud has been told the Devil would be coming for her. With only her schizophrenic mother to protect her, Mud must learn to survive in the swamps of Louisiana by any means necessary.

Even if she must take a life to do it.

But then her mother is murdered in front of her...

Suddenly alone in the world, Mud takes to the streets, stealing what's required to stay alive. She knows that evil is coming, and she trusts no one. Until a chance meeting with Grace Holloway changes everything. Grace seems kind and generous, taking Mud in when no one else would. But Grace's life is also filled with secrets—dark secrets that could very well destroy them both...

The Girl Who Lived to Tell

A Chilling Thriller

Blurb:

How far would you go to stay alive?

Sandy Patterson has it all: a handsome husband who adores her and a new job teaching math at the local high school. But a dark cloud hangs over the halls. A serial killer stalks the shadows, snatching innocent teenage girls and leaving behind a string of broken and battered corpses. Not even the FBI can find this elusive murderer.

Until one fateful night, Sandy finds herself in the clutches of the same psychotic maniac who wants nothing more than to torture and demean her. Forced into a mind-bending game of life and death, Sandy races to unlock the mystery surrounding her twisted captor. But time is running out for her — and her unborn baby. To survive, she'll have to learn to think like a killer. Or become one herself…

Quick Chronicles

A Gripping Thriller Series

The Silencer – Book 1

Blurb:

Six bodies. Two serial killers. And a profiler with nothing left to lose.

Some demons refuse to stay buried. Especially when it's personal. Former FBI profiler, Oliver Quick, has spent the past six years obsessed with catching a serial killer known as the Silencer. But the trail's gone cold.

Until the FBI asks for his help on a case involving a mutilated woman found beneath the pier of a local tourist attraction.

The chase is on, with Oliver hunting not one but two serial killers. The Silencer is back, and he's toying with Quick.

Oliver finds himself trapped in a deadly game of cat-and-mouse with one of the most notorious serial killers to ever live. Will he finally catch the Silencer and put his demons to rest, or is the Hunter about to become the Hunted…

The Prophet – Book 2

Silence of the Whippoorwill

A Psychological Thriller

Blurb:

Vengeance is mine...

Legend has it, when the whippoorwill sings, death is soon to follow...

But Investigator Breezy Anderson doesn't believe in myths. Until a hiking trip to the mountains of Arkansas with some friends, takes a dangerous turn.

Breezy soon discovers, they're not alone. A group of crazed psychopaths are hunting them, picking them off one by one. With no hope of escape, Breezy is forced into a cat-and-mouse game of death and survival.

About Ditter

Ditter Kellen is the USA Today Bestselling Author of Mystery-Thriller-Suspense-Christian Thriller Novels. She loves spinning edgy, heart-pounding stories that will leave you guessing until the very end.

A devoted wife, mother and Christian, Ditter resides in Florida with her husband, teenage son, and many unique farm animals.

She adores French fries and her phone is permanently attached to her ear. You can contact Ditter by email: ditterkellen@outlook.com

But her attackers made one mistake. They left her alive...

The Hitcher

A Heart-Pounding Thriller